WAR AND PEAS

WAR AND PEAS

• • • • •

JILL CHURCHILL

AVON BOOKS ◆ NEW YORK

For Tom and Mary Wright,
the best first readers in the world

WAR AND PEAS is an original publication of Avon Books. This work has never before appeared in book form. This work is a novel. Any similarity to actual persons or events is purely coincidental.

AVON BOOKS
A division of
The Hearst Corporation
1350 Avenue of the Americas
New York, New York 10019

Copyright © 1996 by The Janice Young Brooks Trust
Author photograph by Ken Clark
Interior book design by Kellan Peck
Published by arrangement with the author
Library of Congress Catalog Card Number: 96-23384
ISBN: 0-380-97323-5

Library of Congress Cataloging in Publication Data:
Churchill, Jill.
  War and peas / Jill Churchill.
     p.   cm.
I. Title.
PS3553.H85W3   1996   96-23384
813´.54—dc20   CIP

First Avon Books Hardcover Printing: November 1996

AVON TRADEMARK REG. U.S. PAT. OFF. AND IN OTHER COUNTRIES, MARCA REGISTRADA, HECHO EN U.S.A.

Printed in the U.S.A.

FIRST EDITION

Q 10 9 8 7 6 5 4 3 2 1

Chapter 1

1863—Sort of

Jane Jeffry shifted the heavy gunnysack to her other shoulder and almost stumbled. The field was rutted and the stubble of last year's wheat crop dragged at the hem of her calico dress and poked at her legs through her prickly black wool stockings. Her feet hurt in her tightly laced shoes, but they were the only things keeping her ankles from collapsing. It was so hot. She and her friend Shelley could have walked to town along the dusty track at the edge of the field: it would have been shadier and easier walking, but there were dangers in the woods. Desperate men with hair-trigger tempers, empty bellies, and eyes and hands starved for the sight and feel of women. No, it wasn't safe to walk near the woods where soldiers—or worse, deserters—might be hiding. If only she'd worn a bonnet with a wider brim to keep the sun off her face.

There were other women making the long trek to town for supplies as well. Jane looked over her shoulder and could tell that the threesome a few yards behind was suffering, too. Their postures were wary but exhausted, and one rather plump young woman had a face as red as a beet.

Jane glanced past Shelley at the inviting shade and wished they'd thought to bring water along. "I'm thirsty," Jane complained.

"It's not much farther," Shelley said. She, too, was suffering from the heat. The ties of her bonnet were sweat-soaked and she was squinting against the bright August day. "It's too bad ladies can't go into the saloon in town. But there's that pump in front of the saddler's. We can get a drink there."

They stumbled on for a few more feet and Shelley suddenly stopped, putting her hand out to signal Jane to listen. There was the faint sound of a bugle.

"What does that mean?" Jane asked.

"I don't know," Shelley said, "except that we'd better hurry."

Glancing nervously at the woods on either side of the field, they hitched up their long skirts and layers of petticoats and tried to make better speed. But it was useless. Before they'd gone a few yards, they heard men shouting.

"Over there," Jane gasped, pointing to their right.

"No, the other way," Shelley countered, gesturing toward the grove of trees to their left.

Suddenly the field was overrun by soldiers: Confederate to one side of them, tearing across the field; Union to the other, firing from the woods. The bloodcurdling sound of rebel yells laced through the sharp cracks of gunfire and the screams of the women trying to flee for safety. But there was no escape. They were surrounded, trapped between two clashing armies. A Confederate soldier with a sword dashed past them and part of Jane's brain registered how tattered and sad, yet fanatic, he looked with his patched uniform, untrimmed beard, and flashing eyes. Jane felt her throat closing from the hot, acrid scent of gunpowder. She dropped her heavy pack—it was the tomatoes she'd grown to trade for flour for the winter.

"Here! This way," Shelley shouted about the noise. Dying men were screaming with pain. A boy no more than thirteen had carried the regimental flag onto the field and was now sprawled across it facedown. They stepped over him and ran toward the town. One of the women who'd been walking behind them had somehow gotten ahead of them and had fallen, too. Her straw hat with the sun-faded cloth cabbage roses was twisted around, concealing her face.

Shelley fell in a rut and almost went down on her knees, but Jane grabbed her by the arm and dragged her forward. They had to keep their eyes on the ground to stop from falling again.

Jane looked up just in time to prevent them from running right into a crowd of people wearing shorts and tank tops, and sitting on aluminum lawn chairs.

They were applauding.

Shelley skidded to a stop, looked down at her arms, which were scratched and dirty. "It's going to take a week at Elizabeth Arden to get over this," she said.

According to the brochure that was being handed out after the reenactment, Auguste Caspar Snellen had come from Alsace-Lorraine to the Chicago area as an ambitious boy of twenty in 1875. Just north of the city, he'd claimed a large parcel of land that turned out to be one of those microclimates that were sensational for growing peas. He'd tried potatoes first, but they rotted. Rutabagas grew well, but nobody wanted them. Corn withered on the stalk. But when he tried his hands at peas, they flourished as if by magic. Being of an amateur scientific bent, Auguste started importing other varieties of peas. They turned to gold. Rather than selling the peas as food, he sold them as seed all over the country. He built a little laboratory and greenhouse and developed new strains. By the time he was fifty, Auguste Snellen was the "Pea King" and a very wealthy man.

In 1907, he used some of his wealth to endow a museum, which was named for him. He'd originally wanted the museum to be filled solely with exhibits having to do with the history and significance of peas, which he found endlessly fascinating, but he was finally persuaded that other agricultural (and eventually domestic) pursuits were also fit subjects for museum exhibits.

Auguste Snellen was responsible for the county's Pea Festival, which had taken place every August (no coincidence, that) since 1927—except in 1945, when everybody was too busy celebrating the end of the war; and in 1964, when a tornado ripped through the fairgrounds the afternoon before the opening of the festival and scattered jellies, afghans, flower exhibits, farm implements, and a few startled piglets far and wide.

The Snellen Museum always had a "presence" at the Pea Festival, but for years it was usually a single booth with a few dusty artifacts and boring hand-labeled signs inviting people to visit the museum to see more of the same. But ten years earlier, there had been a change. The booth was enlarged, and the exhibits grew more interesting and more professionally presented. This was because of Regina Price Palmer, the then very young woman who had been appointed director of the Snellen Museum, and Lisa Quigley, the publicity director Regina had urged the board to hire.

The women were a perfect pair, united in their vision of the Snellen's future. And this year the Snellen Museum, under their guidance, had promoted itself in a big way at the Pea Festival. They'd rented a huge tent, put together a truly impressive exhibit, including a real sod house, and done an enormous amount of advance advertising for the Civil War reenactments they were sponsoring ("BE A PART OF YOUR OWN HISTORY—EVERY DAY AT 10 A.M. AND 2 P.M.").

Jane fanned herself with the brochure and looked longingly at an empty lawn chair in a shady spot under a maple tree near the edge of the field. Surely its owner wouldn't mind letting a hot, sweaty, itchy reenactor sit down for a minute or two. If she snagged the empty chair, however, she wouldn't be able to go find a cold drink, but if she went for a drink first, the lawn chair might become occupied. Funny how her brain didn't quite work in the heat. How on earth had women survived summer in this kind of garb?

"Jane, that was great," Mel VanDyne said from behind her.

"Oh, Mel! Thank God! I can sit down. Would you please, please get me something cold to drink? And maybe a bucket of ice water to slosh over me while you're at it?"

She flung herself into the chair and watched as he walked away. Mel was her "significant other" (a term she'd reluctantly adopted because her teenage daughter, Katie, thought

it was inappropriate for a mother to have a "boyfriend").
He was also a detective, but at the moment, he was merely
the object of all her gratitude. While she waited, trying not
to pant, she glanced around for Shelley, who had disappeared and was probably hiding from her. And well she
should. Shelley had volunteered the two of them, not only
for the reenactment, but for a couple weeks' worth of time
at the museum.

Mel returned with a huge plastic cup full of lemonade
and another of ice water. Jane knocked back a few big swal-
lows of the lemonade in a most unladylike way, then fished
an ice cube out of the water to rub on her neck.

"I don't think you'd have been suited to the pioneer life,"
Mel said mildly, watching her make a dripping mess of
herself.

"It was nice of you to come out and watch. What are
those people doing, staying out in the field?" she added. A
group of soldiers and the women who had been behind her
and Shelley during the early part of the reenactment were
huddled in a knot. Some were kneeling.

Mel looked in that direction for a minute; then Jane noticed him stand a little straighter.

"I think there's something wrong," he said quietly.

Jane stood up and could see that there was someone or
something lying on the ground. "Uh-oh. Do you think someone really did have a heat stroke?"

As she spoke, one of the women in the group suddenly
broke away and started running toward them. She was tearing along at full tilt and as she got near where Jane and Mel
were standing, she tripped over her skirts. Mel grabbed her
to break her fall.

"I have to call an ambulance!" she cried.

"Sit down here before you collapse," Mel said, leading her to the chair Jane had abandoned. "I'll call for you." He reached into his back pocket and pulled out a mobile phone Jane hadn't known he was carrying.

"What happened?" Jane asked.

The woman, clad in the same kind of heavy, hot garments Jane was wearing, was red-faced and gulping for breath. "It's Ms. Palmer. I think she's dead!"

"Oh, no!" Jane exclaimed. "Surely she just fainted from the heat!"

"No!" The younger woman was sobbing now. "No, she's been shot!"

Chapter2

Mel gestured at Jane to keep the young woman where she was. Jane nodded and Mel turned away so he could speak without being heard. Jane handed over the remains of her glass of lemonade to the woman. "Take a long drink. You look ready to fall down yourself. That's Detective VanDyne calling. He'll take care of everything. Just relax for a minute so you can calm down and cool off."

The young woman, still sobbing, tried to drink, hiccuped and choked a bit, then tried again. Her brilliant orange-red hair had been pulled into a tiny bun at the back of her head, but had come loose and was frizzed around her face, which was now drenched with sweat and as pale as an eggshell. Jane was afraid she might be going into shock. She grabbed a brochure someone had dropped on the ground and started fanning her charge with both hands.

The young woman took several gulps, a couple of deep breaths, and her color improved. "I'm sorry I acted so hysterical," she finally said. "Thank you for the drink."

WAR AND PEAS

"I'm Jane Jeffry. I don't think we met before the reenactment."

"I'm Sharlene Lloyd. I'm—I *was* Ms. Palmer's secretary."

"Now, now. We don't know for sure yet."

Jane glanced around. Mel had finished his phone call and was striding out across the field. Several people were staring at Sharlene and many more were wandering about. "Sharlene, are your regular clothes in that house trailer where my friend and I got dressed?" Sharlene nodded. "Then let's go cool off and get our own clothes on."

"I can't. I should be helping."

"There's nothing we can do right now, and you'll need your wits about you later. Come on," Jane insisted.

She took Sharlene's arm and led her through the fairgrounds. Along the way, she spotted Shelley, who joined them and whispered, "What happened?"

Jane put a finger to her lips and muttered, "Later."

The mobile home the museum had rented for the staff's use was parked in a shady spot behind the Pea Pod Ride, an ancient, creaking mechanism with baskets fashioned to look like pea pods. The mobile home was large, luxurious, and must have been specially selected for the power of its air-conditioning system; for as the three women entered, they were engulfed in what seemed to them, after being outside, like frigid air. Sharlene picked through the grocery bags neatly lined up on the sofa for the one with her name on it in red.

"Do you think it's okay if I use the shower?" she asked.

"I'd say it was mandatory," Jane replied with an encouraging grin.

Sharlene smiled weakly and disappeared into the minuscule bathroom.

"What on earth is going on?" Shelley asked the moment the door had closed.

"Sharlene said someone was shot to death out on that field."

Shelly put her hand over her mouth. "No!"

"She said it was her boss."

"Regina Price Palmer?"

"Yes, Palmer was the name. Who is she?"

"She's the museum director," Shelley replied.

"Oh, of course. Her name was in the brochure. That's why it sounded familiar."

"Is she right?" Shelley asked. "Sharlene's obviously in bad shape herself. Could the heat have made her a little loopy?"

Jane shrugged. "I don't know. But something certainly happened. Someone was on the ground with a crowd standing around looking alarmed."

Just as the faint sound of sirens became audible, there was a sharp knock on the door, and in stepped a young man in farmer's overalls rolled up to his knees, with a straw hat perched on his head of brown hair worn in a long ponytail. "Excuse me, do either of you know where Sharlene Lloyd is?"

"Yes, she's showering and changing," Shelley said.

"She's okay, then? Good." He put out his hand to Jane, who was closest to him. "Jumper Cable," he said.

Jane took his hand. "I'm sorry—I have no idea where you'd find a jumper cable."

"No, that's me."

"You're a jumper cable?" Jane asked with alarm, gingerly

freeing her hand. Had the heat made everyone crazy? Or perhaps she was crazy and imagining this conversation. Soon she'd be thinking she was Napoleon.

"I'm sorry. Tom Cable. People call me Jumper."

Relieved, Shelley and Jane introduced themselves. Jumper said, "I just wanted to make sure Sharlene was okay. Tell her I came by, would you?"

And with that, he was gone. A second later, Sharlene emerged from the bathroom. She had on a denim skirt, a sleeveless white blouse, and sandals; a towel was wrapped around her head. She held her "pioneer woman" clothes in her arms. She was obviously feeling better, at least physically. "I'm sorry. It was rude of me to rush in first like that. I probably used all the hot water, too."

"I hope you have," Shelley said. "I want a cold shower. Oh, a boy calling himself Jumper Cable came to see if you were okay."

Sharlene blushed. "He's not a boy. Tom Cable is the museum's attorney. Thanks for telling me."

"Attorney?" Jane asked. "He looked barely old enough to vote!"

"He does look young," Sharlene said a bit defensively, "but he's thirty-three years old. Last May twelfth."

Shelley picked out her own grocery sack and took her turn in the bathroom. She came out a few minutes later, looking as fresh as new paint. Her short, dark hair was already half dry and as tidy as always. Sharlene went to hang up all their pioneer clothes while Jane got cleaned up. There was no hot water left, as Sharlene had predicted, but the cool shower was refreshing and putting on clean, lightweight cotton clothes was even more so. Jane was still combing out her wet, dark blond mop of hair when Mel arrived.

"I thought I'd never find you!" he exclaimed.

"Sharlene, this is my friend Detective Mel VanDyne," Jane said. "Sharlene Lloyd is Ms. Palmer's secretary."

Sharlene asked, "Is she dead? Really?"

"I'm afraid so, Ms. Lloyd. Do you feel like answering a few questions?"

Sharlene became teary-eyed again. "I think—will you excuse me for a minute?"

She disappeared into the depths of the mobile home, and Mel said to Jane and Shelley, "Then I'll start with you two."

"Are you in charge of the case?" Jane asked.

"No, just helping with interviews. There was a mob of people out there, you know, and it's important to interview as many as possible as quickly as possible."

"I don't know how much help we can be, Mel," Jane said. "We weren't in 'witness' mode."

"People seldom are," he replied.

"But we were really out in left field, if you'll forgive the expression," Shelley put in. "We were busy pretending like mad. The woman who rehearsed us really emphasized that we weren't to try to *act* the parts, but really get into it and *be* the people. She said that was the whole point of a reenactment. And we took her at her word. It was spooky, in fact. I was really scared of the battle, even though I knew it was all fake."

"But unfortunately, it wasn't," Jane added grimly. "Shelley's right. We weren't quite ourselves. Maybe it was just the heat, but I felt—well, almost hypnotized into my part."

Mel wasn't very sympathetic. "Then you're going to have

to snap out of it, because I need information. Do the best you can, okay?"

But it wasn't a successful interview. The experience had been pure chaos and neither of them could satisfactorily choreograph exactly what they'd done in what order, let alone account for anyone else's movements.

"There was a group of women—three of them, I think—just behind us to begin with," Jane summed up. "One of them was Sharlene Lloyd. I remembered her because her red hair and red face made her look so much hotter than the rest of us. And one of the women with her had a hat with cloth flowers like big cabbage roses. I saw her later, when we were trying to escape. She was ahead of us then, though. And she was already lying on the ground. Was that Ms. Palmer?"

Mel nodded. "Did she look injured when you saw her?"

"She looked dead," Shelley said bluntly. "But then, she was supposed to pretend to be dead, I guess."

"You couldn't see her expression," Jane said. "She was facedown and her hat had skewed around and concealed her features."

Sharlene rejoined them. Her nose and eyes were pink and she had a crumpled tissue in her hand, but she was calm. "I've been listening to your questions," she said softly. "I'm afraid I don't know much, either. I was walking with Ms. Palmer and Babs McDonald. And I know it sounds crazy, but I, too, sort of felt like it was really happening. When the shooting started, I just froze. I was worried about Babs—Mrs. McDonald. She's the older lady, you know. Miss Daisy's friend. And I was worried about her being out in the heat or falling and breaking her hip or something. So I

13

just stood there, and when the soldiers got close, Babs gave me a shove and said to run for safety. I turned around and ran back the way we'd come."

"Where was Ms. Palmer then?" Mel asked very gently.

Sharlene sniffed and touched the tissue to her nose. "I don't know. I didn't look. I was only thinking about myself."

Mel nodded and said, "Of course you were. That's understandable. What happened next?"

"Well, I ran a few feet and a soldier almost ran into me. He yelled something about getting out of the way and threw me to the ground. No, not really threw me, but he made it look like that. So I just stayed there, playing possum."

"Could you see the others?" Mel asked.

"No, I was in a low spot."

"Had someone told you to run back that way? Was it planned?"

"No, not really." Sharlene spoke more firmly now. "I believe the actual reenactors have what they do pretty well planned. But those of us from the museum were just extras. We were there for a little extra 'color' and were only told about how we were supposed to imagine we were walking to town and no matter what happened, to act like the person we were pretending to be would probably have acted."

Shelley and Jane nodded their agreement, and Shelley added, "As part of the museum's function, the woman in charge told us a lot about the clothes we were wearing and how we would have lived, and suggested 'roles.' I was the town minister's wife—" She looked warningly at Jane, as if her friend might make another joke about that, but Jane kept a straight face and Shelley continued. "And Jane was my cousin whose family had come out to homestead next to our farm. We were taking our tomatoes to market to trade for flour. They made us carry gunnysacks of real tomatoes so we'd know how heavy they were."

Mel nodded. "Excuse me for wandering off track for a minute," he said to Sharlene, "but I don't recall any Civil War battles around here. I'm not much of a history buff, but—"

"It wasn't meant to be a real battle," Sharlene said. Again she was speaking of something about which she was knowledgeable, and her voice and manner were more confident. "Only to give the flavor of what it was like. Lisa Quigley— she does all our publicity and promotion at the Snellen—set it up, so I don't know a whole lot about it, but I think the reenactors—the real ones—based it on some actual battle that took place in Tennessee. They have a club here in Chicago and they like to do this whenever they can. I think some of them spend a fortune on their uniforms and equipment and all, and travel long distances to go to actual sites. But they all have real jobs and can't do that very often, I imagine. They're very picky about accuracy otherwise. Even their underwear and the toothbrushes in their packs are either antique items or exact reproductions. That's why the museum is so strict with the extras. We can't use bobby pins in our hair or wear makeup. And we have to wear wool stockings like the people did then. I'm sorry. I guess you don't care about all that right now."

"I don't know what I care about," Mel said with an encouraging smile. "I'm just collecting information. You seem to have a lot of it."

"Well, I've worked at the museum since I finished secretarial school," Sharlene said modestly. "I've picked things up."

"Tell me about the museum, then," Mel said.

Sharlene briefly repeated what was in the brochure Jane had read earlier. "Miss Daisy Snellen inherited all her grandfather's money that he made from peas. When she died a couple years ago, she left most of it to the museum board of directors. It had grown to around ten million dollars."

Mel whistled softly.

Sharlene nodded agreement. "Most of it was invested, and part of it was used to hire an architect to—" She stopped suddenly. "Oh, Mr. Abbot! Poor Mr. Abbot!"

"Who's that?" Jane asked.

"Ms. Palmer's fiancé. He was the architect who was hired to make the plans for a new museum building. And he and Ms. Palmer fell in love and were supposed to be married this winter. Oh, no! How terrible for him! Somebody has to tell him!"

"I'm sure someone's told him about it already," Mel said.

"Or asked him," Shelley muttered under her breath to Jane.

"I have to talk to the others," Sharlene said. "Lisa and poor Mr. Abbot. May I go now? Everybody's going to be so upset, and we're supposed to have the groundbreaking ceremony tomorrow. Oh, dear!"

Mel nodded, thanked her for her information, and warned her that he'd probably have more questions for her later on.

When she'd gone, Jane said, "We'd better get out of here. Everybody's going to be wanting to change. Mel, what happened out there? Was the woman really shot?"

"It looks like it. And damned near everybody out there

had guns. One poor guy is trying to collect them all now and the reenactors aren't happy about turning over their weapons. We can't require them to, only ask them to do so voluntarily, of course, and since most of the weapons are valuable antiques or expensive replicas, many reenactors aren't feeling especially cooperative. It's a mess."

"Can you tell if she was shot up close or at a distance?" Jane asked.

"That'll be for the coroner's office to determine, but there weren't any visible powder burns."

"At least you're not in charge," Jane said with an attempt to cheer him up.

"Jane, I'm out in the middle of nowhere on what is probably the hottest day of the year, if not the hottest day in recorded history, and I'm trying to be authoritative and official while wearing shorts and a silly green T-shirt that says, 'The Best Pea-Pickin' Festival in the World.' Not being 'in charge' isn't much comfort."

"But you've got great legs," Jane said, unimpressed by his complaints.

He glared at her for a minute, then laughed. "I do, don't I?"

Chapter**3**

Jane and Shelley went to the Snellen booth, where a couple of museum volunteers wearing pea-green T-shirts were anxious to be relieved. They were also desperately eager to know what all the sirens and police were about, but Shelley and Jane pleaded ignorance.

The booth not only was shaded, it had aluminum lawn chairs and, more important, a big floor fan humming along under the counter that made everything almost pleasant. Shelley set to work sorting out and stacking up the brochures, which were randomly spread all over the counter. Jane tidied up the sale items—little enamel pea-pod lapel pins and matching earrings, peashooters, jump ropes that were a string of green plastic peas with pod handles, and ceramic dishes with ceramic peas and carrots. There were necklaces made of dried, shellacked peas that were actually rather pretty, and a Chinese checkers game with brightly painted peas for players that wasn't pretty at all. And there were a great many of the green Pea Pickin'

T-shirts like the ones Jane had unwisely persuaded Mel to wear.

"Did you know this Palmer woman?" Jane asked Shelley as they finished their work and sat down to wait for customers.

"Not well. We'd met when I started working as a volunteer at the museum, and I'd seen her around. Probably hadn't exchanged more than a hundred words with her."

"Did she strike you as the type of person somebody would want to kill?"

"You think it was deliberate?" Shelley asked. "Surely it was just an accident."

"I don't see quite how it could be. Like Mel said, everybody had guns out there, but none of them were supposed to have real bullets. I don't know anything about guns, but I wouldn't think anybody who knew about them could mistake a blank for a bullet."

"I think you can get killed with blanks, too," Shelley said. "Maybe that's what happened. And to answer your question, no. She seemed like a very nice, bland person. In fact, my impression was that she was one of those earnest, boring individuals who use all their energy to do their job very well and have nothing left to form a personality."

"So she was really good at being a museum director? What does that entail?"

"I've no idea," Shelley said. "Administrative stuff, I guess. But everybody at the museum deferred to her with what seemed like real respect. I know she managed to bag a couple of traveling exhibits that were a big deal in museum circles. Well, in little pea-museum circles, at any rate. And she was in charge of getting the new building and organizing the move. Which is why I dragged you in, Jane."

"We're moving things next week? But, Shelly, there's nowhere to move to. The ground-breaking for the new building is tomorrow. Or it was supposed to be."

"Jane, the museum's been in the same building since 1907. The basement alone is stacked with ninety years' worth of— stuff. People give their old junk to museums and it piles up. It all has to be cataloged and evaluated and packed up for the move when the building is ready. It's months and months of work. I imagine half of the stuff, at least, will just be pitched. Or given to some even more downtrodden museum."

"But, Shelley, I'm antiques-impaired. I don't know valuable from dreck. And you're not much brighter than I am about it."

"We don't have to make decisions. Just write down what we can recognize, store it in boxes with labels, and leave everything else for the experts."

"You're saying we're the bottom of the food chain, aren't you? The poor slobs who dust things off and sweep up the mouse droppings?"

"Just about. But it's the necessary first step."

"And we start that on Monday? How long is our sentence?"

"I only volunteered you for next week," Shelley said. "I knew you'd be busy the week after that, getting Mike off to college."

Jane almost offered the comment that her son Mike was doing quite nicely at preparing himself for college, but feared that might get her condemned to yet another week in a dusty, musty basement. For the past two weeks he'd been taking his own inventory of possessions, passing down many of his treasures to his soon-to-be-seventh-grade brother, Todd, and high-schooler-sister, Katie. To give them credit, they received his offerings with a polite pretense of gratitude. Mike had also generated a mountain of trash. His bedroom was eerily tidy now, with most of his belongings stored in cartons in the garage, ready to be put in the back of his brand-new, graduation-gift pickup truck and Jane's wheezing old station wagon when moving day arrived.

A day Jane dreaded.

Since her husband had died in a car accident several years earlier, Jane's practical, sensible oldest child had been her mainstay. She was realizing the truth of something her mother often said: that about the time your kids get to be real people whom you like, they go away.

"Quit daydreaming," Shelley said. "I think we have a customer."

A man was approaching, slapping a Snellen Museum brochure against the palm of his hand. He was plump and vaguely unhealthy-looking, with graying blond hair and a sparse Douglas Fairbanks-style mustache. He wore baggy plaid shorts and a Snellen Museum Pea Pickin' T-shirt that was much too tight. He strolled along the length of the counter, critically surveying the merchandise, picking things up, setting them down, shaking his head as if angry.

Shelley asked him cheerfully if there was anything in particular he wanted, and he merely grunted a rude negative. After examining everything, he said to her, "So what do you sell this junk for?"

Shelley's eyes flashed, but she answered pleasantly. "The prices are marked on each item."

"Yeah, but what does the museum make on each thing? What percentage?"

Shelley drew herself up indignantly. "I have no idea. Nor can I imagine why you need to know."

He wasn't cowed. "I'm interested 'cause I'm a Snellen, lady. My family funds this operation."

But Shelley wasn't easily intimidated, either. "Then you surely have access to that information without being rude to a volunteer."

"Yeah, I'll ask Georgia. She'll know." And without any apology, he shambled off.

"What a jerk!" Shelley muttered.

Sharlene Lloyd came through the tent flap at the back of the booth. "Is he gone?" she asked quietly.

"The Nightmare Customer? Yes, he's gone. Who is he?" Shelley asked.

"He's Miss Daisy Snellen's nephew, Caspar. He's always giving somebody trouble. Was he nasty to you?"

"Only moderately," Shelley admitted. "Nothing I couldn't handle."

"I came to see if you've had anything to eat," Sharlene said. "I'll get you some lunch."

"No, no!" Jane said. "If you'll sit and rest a minute here with Shelley, I'll get us something. You don't have to wait on us."

"But the volunteers are supposed to be fed at Snellen expense and I need—"

"Have you had anything to eat, Sharlene?" Jane cut in. "No? Well, I'll get everybody something and we'll sort it out with the museum later." She got up and practically forced Sharlene into her vacant chair. When Jane returned a few minutes later with hot dogs, chips, a few limp celery stalks, and drinks, Shelley was waiting on a customer and Sharlene was reorganizing the small cash box.

Shelley sent her customer off with two museum bumper stickers and a jump rope, then sat down. "That's appalling, Jane," she said, staring at Jane's hot dog, which was piled high with sauerkraut and suspiciously yellow cheese. "How can you eat something so revolting?"

"I've got a cast-iron digestive track," Jane said. "Except I'm starting to have a little trouble with melons—"

"I don't want to hear about it!" Shelley said firmly. "Sharlene, what about the groundbreaking ceremony tomorrow? Will it go on?"

"I don't know. I guess it's up to Babs McDonald and Tom."

It took Jane a second to remember that "Tom" was Jumper Cable, the attorney who looked like an eighteen-year-old. "Why them in particular?"

"Because they're the most important people on the board of directors of the museum. That's how Miss Daisy Snellen wanted it. At least one of them has to approve any important decision."

Shelley and Jane chatted about the merchandise until Sharlene had finished her food, which she set aside barely nibbled. Shelley said, "Sharlene, can you talk about Ms. Palmer? I hardly knew her at all."

Sharlene's eyes filled with tears, but she lifted her head and said, "She was wonderful. Just the most wonderful person in the world. At least to me she was. When I started working at the museum, I'd just finished my secretarial course. I knew how to type and take shorthand, but I didn't know much about spelling and grammar because I always thought that was dull. Ms. Palmer would correct my mistakes without making me feel stupid. All my teachers had always made out like I was some kind of dummy. I was real pretty in high school, and I guess they expected me to be an idiot."

"You're very pretty now," Jane said, "and you're obviously not stupid."

"No, I'm fat."

"You're voluptuous," Shelley exclaimed. "I'd give anything for a bosom like yours!"

Sharlene blushed and said, "Voluptuous? I'll look that one up. Anyway, after a while, Ms. Palmer told me about some classes I could take in English. Didn't say I had to, or even that I needed to. Just made it sound like something I'd have fun doing. And, you know? It was. Everybody else in the class carried on like crazy about having to diagram sentences and all, but I liked it. It was like working jigsaw puzzles, sort of."

Jane nodded. "I liked it, too."

"Ms. Palmer always asked about what I was learning, and even helped me when there was something I didn't understand. She was awfully smart and well educated. Went to fancy private schools, I imagine. Anyhow, after I took those classes, she started talking about other classes I could take. History and business. She even got the board of directors to pay for my tuition. On-the-job training, she called it. When I got my certificate from junior college . . ." She paused, a sob stuck in her throat for a minute, then took a deep breath and plowed on. "When I got my certificate, there was a ceremony. Ms. Palmer not only came to it, but she brought Babs McDonald and even Miss Daisy Snellen, who hardly went out at all by that time. It was like having a family there that was proud of me."

Jane was getting choked up herself. "How lovely!" she said in a shaky voice. "And how proud of you they all must have been."

Sharlene nodded. "I think they really were."

Shelley, considerably less sentimental than Jane, said, "Sharlene, you said she was wonderful to you. I see what you mean, but did everybody like her as much as you did?"

"Everybody respected and admired her. Well—almost everyone."

"Who didn't?" Shelley asked bluntly.

Sharlene waved toward the front of the booth. "That awful Caspar Snellen, the man who was just here. He didn't like her at all, but that was his own fault."

"Why didn't he like her?" Jane asked.

"Oh, because he's mean and greedy. Miss Daisy Snellen was his aunt, you see. And he thought he and his sister, Georgia, should get all the Snellen money. When Miss Daisy died, she left him and his sister a lot of money. About a million dollars each, I heard. But the rest all went to the museum. And Caspar made a big, hateful stink about it. Said Ms. Palmer had sucked up to his aunt and that Miss Daisy was senile. It was awful. He brought some kind of lawsuit and threatened to have newspaper interviews and everything. In fact, he'd done something nasty even before Miss Daisy died."

"What kind of something?" Shelley asked.

"Tried to have her declared incontinent—no, incompetent. I mix those words up. But Tom took care of that in no time."

"Was Tom Cable Miss Daisy's attorney?" Jane asked, having a lot of trouble picturing Jumper Cable in a suit and tie, arguing a case in court.

Sharlene nodded. "And he was like an honorary grandson to her, too."

"So Miss Snellen's nephew, Caspar, was the only person who disliked Ms. Palmer?" Shelley persisted.

"As far as I know. Well, there's Derek, too. But he doesn't like anyone."

"Who in the world is Derek?" Jane asked.

"He's the assistant director of the museum. When Miss Daisy died and the board decided to build the new building and all, they thought it would be too hard for Ms. Palmer to do everything and insisted that it was time to get an assistant director."

"Why did Derek dislike her?"

"I shouldn't have said that," Sharlene said. "I don't think Derek disliked her, exactly. He's just real ambitious and I think he wanted her job. And I don't think he liked being second to a woman. He's a real sexist jerk. You know, the kind of man who's always pawing and drooling over women, but you know he really despises them."

"Sharlene, I just realized something," Jane said. "You call everyone by their first name except Ms. Palmer."

Sharlene looked perplexed. "Her first name was Regina."

"But you didn't call her that?"

"Oh, no! I wouldn't ever do that. It would be too personal. She was my boss."

"But so are Tom Cable and Babs McDonald, in a way."

"Yes, but they're different."

"How so?"

Sharlene thought for a minute. "I don't know exactly. Ms. Palmer was so businesslike. And such a lady. Well, so is Babs, but she insisted that I call her by her first name. I'm not sure why it was different with Ms. Palmer."

"Excuse me. How do you get inside?" Mel said from the front of the booth.

Jane was startled. "Oh, Mel. I didn't see you there. Come around the back."

She opened the tent flap and held it for him. He was carrying a canvas tote bag with the Pea Festival logo on it. He sat down on Jane's chair and faced Sharlene. From the tote bag he carefully removed a heavy plastic bag. Holding it by one corner, he laid it on the ground and looked up at Sharlene. "Do you recognize this?"

The plastic bag contained a small gun. It was old, ornate, and looked like a fancy toy. Or one of the "ladies" guns that saloon madams in Western movies always seemed to have concealed in their garters.

Sharlene leaned over to study it. "Yes—at least I've seen one just like it. At the museum. Where did you find it?"

"It was left on the field," Mel said. "In a clump of weeds."

Sharlene sat up very straight and paled. "Is it—is it the gun that killed Ms. Palmer?"

"We don't know yet. Can you come to the museum with me now and see if the one the museum owns is still there?"

Chapter4

When they were alone again, Shelley said, "What was all that about first names?"

"I don't know exactly. It just struck me as odd that she never called her boss by a first name," Jane said. "I couldn't figure out if that said something about Sharlene, or about Regina Palmer."

"Probably both," Shelley replied, picking up their paper plates and plastic cups. "She was introduced to me as Ms. Palmer, come to think of it. And she didn't leap in and invite me to call her Regina. But then, I don't always do that with people, either. I make clear to Paul's employees that I'm Mrs. Nowack. And I imagine that there still are a lot of professional women who prefer to keep a little bit of formality in their business relationships."

"Or she was a cold fish," Jane said.

Shelley smiled. "Right. And keep in mind that Regina was Sharlene's mentor. Almost her idol. You don't call idols by their first names. About that gun Mel had—"

WAR AND PEAS

Jane knew what Shelley was thinking and nodded. "Uh-huh. I wouldn't place a bet on there being two of them."

"Which means someone took it from the museum before the reenactment."

"Someone associated with the museum," Jane finished for her. "Not one of the original reenactors. When we had that lecture about our roles, nobody was supposed to have a gun. We were wives and farmers and wagon-makers and such."

A woman with two children who each seemed to have sixteen grabby, grubby little hands had approached the booth. Shelley hopped up to wait on her and try to keep the children from destroying the neatly arranged merchandise. "Oh, you sell pea seeds," the woman said. "How would you like to plant some of our own peas?" she said in a singsong voice to the kids.

"Peas stink!" the boy said.

"I hate peas!" the girl responded, making an ugly face and snatching a jump rope off the counter.

"Oh, you'll love peas if you grow them yourselves," the mother cooed. "I promise they'll taste yummy."

"Plant them indoors in paper cups," Shelley advised. "They're cute when they come up. Then plant them out by a fence when the weather cools. You might get a crop in the fall." As she spoke, Shelley took the jump rope away from the little girl, who was trying to see how many knots she could tie in it. Shelley held it as if she were considering garroting the child.

They left with several packets of peas. "That little boy stole a peashooter," Jane said.

"I know. I charged her for it and she didn't notice," Shelley said smugly.

"How do you know about growing peas?"

"I had to help the teacher with a fourth-grade science project once. I'm a woman of many parts, Jane. Haven't you noticed?"

"And what do your many parts think about Regina Palmer's death?"

"I think she was murdered."

"Me, too."

Mel called that night as Jane was getting ready for bed. "Sorry I abandoned you," he said.

"It was okay. Shelley brought me home."

"I figured she would."

"I guess you'll be attending the festival again tomorrow?" Jane asked.

"Is that an attempt to ask me subtly about Palmer's death?" Mel said with a laugh.

"Not too subtle, huh? Was it the gun from the museum?"

"Sure it was. The gun and lead shot for it had been in a display case."

"Wasn't it locked?"

"It was supposed to be. It was in a remote room on the third floor, in an exhibit of old clothes and hairbrushes and a bunch of dusty, unidentifiable household objects. No telling how long the gun's been missing. And before you ask, everybody in Greater Chicago had access to the keys to the display case. At least everybody who wandered through the staff area. The keys all hang on a pegboard right inside the door."

"And was it the gun she was shot with?" Jane asked.

"No confirmation yet. But I'm guessing so until I'm told otherwise."

"I thought you weren't in charge of the investigation."

He cleared his throat. "I wasn't. But the guy who *was* in charge took a little break during the afternoon and ate something he shouldn't have. Damned near had to have another ambulance for him."

"It wasn't a hot dog with sauerkraut and awfully yellow cheese, was it?" Jane asked warily.

"Nope. A dessert with a cream filling that had ripened nicely in the heat. Somebody else had to bust the dessert booth, thank God!"

"The weather report said it's supposed to be a lot cooler by tomorrow. That's meant as a comforting comment," Jane said.

"Is it? Will you be there again tomorrow?"

"Shelley and I were supposed to participate in the morning reenactment again. But now—? I guess I'll turn up and work at whatever somebody wants me to do."

Surprisingly, the weatherman had been right. A cold front had moved in during the night, causing just enough rain to freshen the skies and grass and leave behind an achingly blue sky. When Jane and Shelley arrived at the festival grounds, they learned that the reenactment scheduled for the morning was to proceed.

"The police are letting you do it again?" Jane asked Jumper Cable, whom they'd met at the museum's trailer.

Jumper was back in his farm-boy outfit already. "Not only letting us, but insisting on it."

"Oh, a reenactment of a reenactment," Shelley said.

Jumper nodded. "Sunday morning is traditionally the lowest attendance, and they want everybody to do exactly what they did yesterday afternoon."

"Somebody won't. I hope!" Jane said.

"It's going to be a critical audience," Jumper said wryly. "Lisa wants us to be ready in fifteen minutes, so grab your costumes."

Jane and Shelley threw on their farmwife clothing and reported in with the group at the far end of the field. Yesterday one of the real reenactors, a beefy, cheerful man with a mop of curly hair, had given a cheerful talk about their group—why they did this, how they researched their roles and battles, where they got their clothes and accouterments. This morning he was present, but silent and subdued. It was as if a real death in the midst of carefully staged fake carnage had seriously offended his sense of the proprieties.

Lisa Quigley, the museum's publicity director, who had told them their "stories" the day before and urged them to believe in their characters and do their own thing, also seemed like a different person today. She was a slim but sturdy, auburn-haired woman in her mid-thirties. Jane had sensed, at their previous meeting, that Lisa was a self-contained sort of person, unused to being in the limelight. It seemed odd that such an individual would have chosen publicity as a career, but she had clearly done her homework. She'd had a sheaf of notes, which she hadn't needed to consult, and had spoken quietly but with real enthusiasm about her subject. Today she was pale and defeated-looking, and her eyes were puffy, as if she'd been crying.

"I won't pretend this is the same kind of activity we engaged in yesterday," she began when everyone had assembled. "And, to be honest, I find this a distasteful and gruesome thing to do. But the police have insisted, and naturally we're extremely eager to help them discover the cause of Ms. Palmer's death. Anyway—our instructions from them are to reproduce our movements in yesterday's reenactment as closely as we can."

Shelley nudged Jane and tilted her head back toward the festival grounds. There were three police officers, badly disguised as ordinary festivalgoers, waiting with video cameras—one at each side of the field, one at the far end where the other spectators would be.

Lisa Quigley continued. "This is Officer Ridley," she said pointing to a woman wearing the same hat, but not the dress, Regina Palmer had worn the day before. "She's been told everyone's impressions of Ms. Palmer's movements and will try to do as Regina did. If any of you have anything additional to tell her, we have a few minutes still. Otherwise, we'll wait until ten o'clock and begin. It would be best, I think, if you would all try to put yourselves in the same frame of mind you were in before. Keep in mind that we have an audience most of which knows nothing about the tragedy and has just come for a good show."

On this slightly upbeat note, they were dismissed. Everybody pointedly ignored Officer Ridley in her cabbage-rose-adorned bonnet. Sharlene Lloyd approached Jane and Shelley with an older woman in tow, whom she introduced as Babs McDonald.

"On behalf of the board of directors, I want to especially thank you ladies for all your help," Babs said in a voice that sounded much younger than she looked. Jane guessed her to be in her seventies—a trim, tiny woman with thick, startlingly white hair braided into earmufflike rolls on either side of her head. "I understand you filled in my duty time at the museum booth yesterday."

"We were glad to," Jane said. "I'm sure you had more important things on your mind."

Babs nodded. There was a touch of the regal in the movement. "Less cheerful things, certainly. And I understand you're helping us next week with our cataloging."

"If you still want us to," Shelley said.

"Of course we do. In fact, we're going to need more help than ever. The loss of Regina isn't going to deter our aims, only make them more of a challenge."

Jane, a State Department brat who had grown up all over the world, suddenly found herself remembering a boarding school she'd attended in Scotland in her early teens when her father was posted to Edinburgh for six months. It had been the hardest school to leave because of a teacher she adored—a teacher Babs McDonald reminded her of. Like that teacher, Babs had a straight-spined elegance and a precision of speech that was a pleasure to hear. The laugh lines around her eyes kept them from being daunting. Babs was one of those older women who looked and acted as if this were the prime of her life.

"Then you're still having the groundbreaking ceremony early this evening?" Shelley asked.

"Certainly!" Babs said. "It was to be the high point of the festival—at least for the employees and supporters of the Snellen Museum. Lisa, as Regina's oldest and dearest friend, will deliver the speech Regina was to give. And Jumper and

I, as president and vice president of the board, will wield the shovel for the ceremony."

"Line up now," Lisa alerted them.

Jane and Shelley tried their best to duplicate what they'd done and thought and said during the previous reenactment, but like everyone else, their eyes were darting about, watching the others, and their hearts and minds weren't on their characters. The gunshots sounded louder and deadlier today. Everyone's actions were stiff and wary, but every bit as chaotic as on the day before. As Jane and Shelley, playing farmwives trying to flee the battlefield, approached the spot where Regina had been lying, there was nothing but a small yellow flag-type marker. And when they reached the festival end of the field and turned and looked back, Officer Ridley was still standing, alone and ignored, her cabbage-rose hat still firmly atop her head.

Jane felt relief—something superstitious deep in her soul had been half afraid something terrible would happen again. And yet she felt an odd sense of disappointment as well. Not that she'd wanted another tragedy, but she'd hoped that something revealing would occur. In some part of her mind she'd hoped against reason for a Perry Mason-type scene, where someone became so rattled and distraught that he or she confessed dramatically.

Mel was standing a few feet away, shaking his head in irritation. Shelley and Jane approached him, and Jane asked, "You don't think it helped?"

"This was *not* my idea. And no, I don't think it helped at all. We'll study all the tapes, of course, but—"

"If you show them to the others, might somebody see

something that's not right?" Jane said, trying to assuage his frustration.

"Jane, I imagine everybody did exactly what they did yesterday. The only difference is, nobody took aim with a stolen antique gun and shot somebody."

Chapter 5

The groundbreaking ceremony was scheduled for five o'clock. At four-thirty, Shelley started packing up the sale items at their booth and Jane carted them to the mobile home. She found much of the museum staff assembled. Sharlene was tidying and packing up the costumes, and Jumper Cable was attempting, with stunning incompetence, to help her. Babs McDonald was at the miniature dining table, going over some paperwork with Lisa Quigley.

As Jane entered with her boxes, a tremendously good-looking man stood up from the sofa, first to study her, then to offer to help her. His quick up-and-down gaze and approving smile might have been flattering, had they not been so blatantly lecherous.

"Hi, there. I don't think we've met," he said, taking the boxes from her and managing to "accidentally" brush his hand against her breast in the process. "I'm Derek Delano." This was said with a flash of handsomely capped teeth.

"I'm glad to meet you," Jane lied. "I'm Jane Jeffry."

"Another of our wonderful volunteers, no doubt." His tone was clearly patronizing.

Jane wished she could do that haughty-eyebrow thing that Shelley was so good at. "Another volunteer," she said. "But I don't know about wonderful. This box is marked 'Pins, jump ropes, and peashooters,' but we sold out on the peashooters."

"Don't worry. Sharlene will sort it all out," he said.

Jane had taken such an instant dislike to him that she found this insulting to Sharlene, though for all she knew, it was part of Sharlene's job. "And are you a volunteer, too, Derek?" she asked cattily.

His frown lasted only an instant before he laughed condescendingly. "No, I'm the assistant director of the Snellen. For now."

He said the last words in a low voice, but across the way, Babs McDonald's head snapped up and she glared at him. Not awfully diplomatic of him, Jane thought, offering to step into Regina Palmer's shoes so soon.

"For now?" Jane repeated innocently. "What do you mean?"

He replied, a little too loudly, "Only that I'll be happy to do anything the Snellen Museum needs at this time of trouble."

Jane went back to the booth and said, "Shelley, I think you should take the next carton over and meet Derek."

"Who's that?" Shelley said, slapping transparent tape along the lid of a box.

"Oh, just the Snellen Museum's very own sleaze. And a perfect murder suspect."

"What on earth are you blathering about?" Shelley

snapped. The tape hadn't gone on perfectly straight, the way she felt tape was supposed to do. She considered such incidents with inanimate objects as personal insults.

"Take that box over and you'll see."

Shelley returned ten minutes later—walking hard on her heels. "What a creep!" she said with an elaborate shudder. "He called me 'babe.' *Babe!*"

"No!"

"He won't do it again," Shelley said, smiling a little.

Jane repeated his remark about being the assistant director—so far. "Babs heard him, but I wanted to make certain he knew she'd heard it. Do you think we should tell Mel?"

"You can, but I don't think there's any need," Shelley said. "The rest of them in the trailer were treating him like he was Typhoid Mary. I don't think there's any love lost on him at the Snellen."

"But there might be elsewhere," Jane said quietly. "Get a load of that."

She gestured with her shoulder. Derek Delano was approaching the booth with a woman on his arm. She was the essence of the country-club type: stylish clothes that were once called "preppie," a golf tan, costly sunglasses, a surgically enhanced figure and face, and expensively streaked blond hair. And in spite of it all, she looked just old enough to be his mother, though her clinging posture and eyelash batting weren't the least maternal.

"Georgia Snellen," Shelley muttered under her breath.

"Same family, I assume?" Jane hissed back. Shelley nodded.

"Closing up shop, I see," Georgia Snellen said as she released Derek and leaned casually against the corner post of the booth.

Shelley didn't bother to make the obvious reply. "I'm Shelley Nowack. We served on the Philharmonic Committee together a number of years ago."

"Not too many years, I hope," Georgia trilled girlishly. "Are you one of the Evanston Nowacks? Lovely family."

Shelley didn't bother to deny it. She introduced Jane.

There followed an interrogation of Jane's social antecedents, during which Jane let Georgia make some unfounded leaps of belief, and Jane ended up related to both a highly respected family of Harvard philosophy professors and an early, though entirely mythical, Arctic explorer (Shelley's contribution).

"And what relation are you to the gentleman I met yesterday?" Jane asked.

"Georgia is Caspar Snellen's sister," Shelley said wickedly.

But Georgia had learned to deal with this unfortunate circumstance. "Poor old Caspar," she said sadly, but didn't elaborate. It was an effective dismissal of the blood tie, and Jane had to give her credit for it. It managed to imply, in three harmless words, that they all had their crosses to bear, that Caspar was hers, and no doubt Jane and Shelley had batty old aunts who lived under bridges eating canned spaghetti, or a cousin in Leavenworth.

"You girls will be at the groundbreaking ceremony, won't you?" Georgia asked. "Derek and I are just on our way over. You could walk along with us."

"We'll be right behind you," Shelley said. "I have one more box to store."

WAR AND PEAS

Derek and Georgia drifted off, she firmly attached to his arm again. Jane laughed. "Shelley! You actually know that awful woman and never told me about her?"

Shelley grinned. "I didn't think you'd believe it. Honestly, I'd forgotten all about her until I saw her draped all over Derek."

"I should have told her I was related to Teddy Roosevelt on his mother's side," Jane said.

"Are you really?"

"No. But it wouldn't matter," Jane said. "She'd have loved it."

"What I don't 'get' about her," Shelley mused, "is that she's so stereotypically nouveau-riche-acting, but she does come from very old money. At least three generations old, which should be enough. And she had a rich husband, too. Maybe he accounts for it."

"How's that?"

"Well, somebody on the Philharmonic Committee told me her husband was a self-made man in the plumbing-fixtures business. Has some kind of patent on portable-john elements or flush handles or something."

"But he was a Snellen, too?"

"No. When they divorced, she apparently took back her maiden name, of which she's inordinately proud."

Jane nodded. "Rather the granddaughter of the Pea King than the ex-wife of the Toilet Bowl Prince, huh? I'm not sure I wouldn't feel the same way."

In the distance, an unskilled but enthusiastic band struck up a tune. "Oh-ho, we better get over there. Sounds like the ceremony is about to start," Shelley said.

"What about the other carton?"

Shelley looked at her pityingly. "Jane, there *is* no other carton. I just didn't want to trail along behind Georgia and Derek like spear-carriers at the opera."

The site of the new museum was across the road from the festival area. The ceremony was to be the closing event of this year's Pea Festival, and in spite of Regina Palmer's death, the museum staff and volunteers did their best to create a celebratory atmosphere. Rows of folding chairs were set up in front of a raised platform where the speakers were to sit. Around the perimeter, stakes with colorful bunches of helium-filled balloons sported the Snellen Museum name and pea-pod logo. Another booth like the one Shelley and Jane had manned was set up as well to give away brochures and an artist's rendering of the new museum and to sell Snellen mementos.

The ground-breaking at five o'clock was conducted with great decorum and mercifully short speeches. Jane was surprised at how many supporters of the museum actually turned up. Of course, the free ice-cream cones promised at the end probably had something to do with it.

Georgia's and Derek's roles were confined to sitting on the raised platform and being introduced, Derek as assistant director and Georgia Snellen as a member of the board of directors. Babs and Jumper Cable were likewise introduced as president and vice president, respectively, of the board. Lisa Quigley was the first to speak, giving a brief history of the museum in a weary voice in spite of her attempts at sparkling intonations. She lauded architect Whitney Abbot's highly creative and yet practical plans for the new museum and added that he wished her to express his extreme regret at being unable to attend the ceremony. At this, she paused as if she'd lost her place for a moment, then quickly took her seat.

Babs McDonald stepped up to the podium and again welcomed everyone, then made the only reference to Regina Palmer. "Only yesterday, the Snellen Museum lost its guiding hand, but not its guiding spirit," she said in her surprisingly young, musical voice. "In great part Regina Price Palmer, the director for the last ten years, was responsible for us all being here today. We salute her memory and her dedication. And, of course, we also salute Miss Daisy Snellen, whose very generous bequest has made it possible for the Snellen Museum to move into the new century in a new home. We hope everyone has enjoyed the Festival this year. I've seen many familiar faces here from years past. And we fervently hope to see all of you next year at the Festival, when we will be celebrating the opening of our new museum."

It almost sounded like a song, or a battle hymn, the way she said it.

Babs descended from the platform on Jumper's arm—he was clad now in a museum Pea Pickin' T-shirt and khaki trousers, not as formal as the occasion might demand, but certainly appropriate—and the two of them arranged their hands on the shovel handle to lift the first, symbolic bit of earth from the ground. They held the position while photos were taken for the local papers and the museum's newsletter and archives.

Somebody behind them sniffled and Jane turned to see Sharlene. Jane moved over to take an empty seat and gestured at Sharlene to come sit between her and Shelley. When Sharlene quit blowing her nose and wiping her eyes, Jane said, "Sharlene, I know it's awfully soon to say this, but you must keep in mind that this is a new, exciting era for the Snellen. I know you're very sad about Ms. Palmer, but think how pleased she would be if she were here today."

"I know. It's not so much that I miss her, even though I do. It's Mr. Abbot I feel so sorry for."

"The building architect? Why?"

"Because they were engaged."

"Oh, that's right," Jane said.

"Well, not exactly engaged. I mean, they'd been sort of engaged a couple times, but I think they were planning to announce at this ceremony that they were really and truly engaged. And now she's dead and he couldn't even stand to come." She dissolved in tears again.

Jane patted her shoulder helplessly. Shelley said, "Sort of engaged? Why 'sort of'?"

Jane handed Sharlene another tissue. Sharlene mopped her eyes and said, "I don't know exactly. They'd dated off and on ever since they started working together. Business lunches and things at first, then real dates. And once, they even went up to Wisconsin for the weekend. But after that they didn't see each other for a while except at the office. At least I don't think they did, and I kept Ms. Palmer's schedule for her. Even her personal meetings."

"What was the problem?" Shelley asked bluntly.

Sharlene shrugged. "I don't know. But it made Mr. Abbot awfully unhappy. Anybody could tell that."

"Didn't you ever ask her?" Jane asked.

Sharlene was horrified. "Oh, no! I would never have done that! It was personal."

Jane thought for a minute. "Maybe she was just reluctant to give up her freedom, do you think? I believe a lot of professional women with good jobs are."

"Maybe," Sharlene said. "But I don't think Mr. Abbot would have expected her to quit working. He was really proud of her."

Shelley had been listening silently, but now asked, "Did you tell the police about Ms. Palmer's schedule book?"

"No. Why would they care about that?" Sharlene replied.

"Because," Jane said gently, "somebody shot her. Maybe somebody in that book."

Chapter 6

Jane arrived at the museum at ten the next morning. Normally she and Shelley would have shared a ride, but Shelley had an early-morning dental appointment. Jane used her friend's absence as an excuse to avoid going directly to work and strolled around the ground floor of the museum for a few minutes before reporting in. She'd been there before, of course, but only as a room mother—a.k.a. unpaid security guard—accompanying various grade-school classes. On those visits her attention had been fully on the children—keeping them from getting lost or handling things they shouldn't touch. She hadn't had time to notice the exhibits.

It was quite a charming place, now that she was able to really look at it. The museum was badly overstuffed, but she liked old-fashioned museums that were crowded with alcoves and dead ends full of surprises. There was, no doubt, a lot to be said for the more modern facilities with plenty of open space and displays featuring a single, well-explained item, but Jane personally preferred the garage-sale look.

WAR AND PEAS

As she was examining a Victorian Hair Wreath, which was both fascinating and revolting, she noticed Casper Snellen standing in the doorway of the room. He was obviously looking for someone, but his gaze passed over her as if she were merely another dusty display. To her relief, he turned on his heel and left. A few minutes later, Sharlene came into the room carrying a posterboard. Jane oozed around behind a piece of farm machinery out of sight. She wanted a few more minutes of just looking around before starting to work. Sharlene was intent on making a bit of room for setting up the poster and didn't even look in Jane's direction.

"Hello? Do you work here?" an older man's voice said.

"Yes, sir, I do. Can I help you?"

Jane peeked out from behind the machinery. The man was a dapper elderly individual in a retirement "uniform"—golf shirt, polyester trousers, and a soft khaki hat.

"Well, no. But I wanted to talk to someone here. My wife and I are doing a little traveling. Got a brand-new mobile home, you see. Visiting our daughter and her kids while they're out of school for the summer. And I've always wanted to come here."

"How nice," Sharlene said with apparently sincere warmth.

After a rather lengthy monologue on the joys of motor homes, retirement, and grandchildren, with a mercifully short excursion into Medicare injustices, the elderly man got to the point. "See, I was a boy in Arkansas during the Depression and have never forgotten Snellen's Little Beauty."

"Little Beauty?" Sharlene asked. "I don't think I've heard of—"

"Oh, you wouldn't have. You're much too young. But old

Snellen sold it back in the early thirties. My old man was a farmer then. He got a couple bags of the seed and tried it out. It was the funniest-lookin' pea plant you ever did see. Supposed to be a bushy variety, but it just laid on the ground. Real green and pretty and had lots of peas, but you couldn't harvest the damned things without crawlin' around on your hands and knees. Mind you, in those days we didn't mind too much crawlin' for food."

"I'm sorry to hear that," Sharlene said politely.

"Don't be. Wasn't a complaint. See, that's not the end of the story I wanted to tell you folks. My old man ordered three or four bags of seed, but forgot one of them and left it in the barn. Next summer he planted potatoes instead and came across this one bag of peas left over from the year before. Too dry and old to eat, but he wasn't one to let anything go to waste. It was dust-bowl days, you know. And those durned peas really grew like mad even in dry ground, which is odd for peas, so after he got his spuds in the ground, he threw the last bag of peas around 'em. Just to hold the soil down, don't you see? Well, I tell you, little lady, we had the biggest, best potatoes in the world that year. You could make a fine meal on just one of them. I can still remember how great they were. We didn't have any butter—my mother would make gravy with a dab of bacon drippings. Never had as good a spud the rest of my life. Well, my old man didn't know much about science, but he could tell a good crop when he saw one. He figured the peas had something to do with it."

"And did they?" Sharlene asked.

"I dunno. But he had all us kids out in that field that fall on our hands and knees picking every last pea. Three years in a row he used those peas for ground cover. Put 'em around beets and turnips and carrots and they grew like crazy. Saw us through bad times, those Little Beauty peas did. Then we lost them."

"Lost them?"

"Late frost. Killed every last plant before it could set flowers."

"Oh, no! Why didn't he get some more?"

"He tried. Boy, oh, boy, did he ever try. Went around to neighbors he'd shared a few seeds with, but theirs had all died, too. Even wrote to old Mr. Snellen himself, telling him about them and asking for more, but he got a letter back saying the company had quit selling them when folks had complained the first year about not being able to pick the things."

"What a shame," Sharlene said.

"I reckon it was. Anyway, I've thought back on those years a lot lately. Guess it's part of getting old. You start remembering your childhood. So when I saw an ad for a Pea Festival in the paper last week and saw the name Snellen, I recalled those peas and wanted to come tell someone here about them."

"I'm so glad you did. That's a wonderful story," Sharlene said. "Would you have the time to come to my office and let me make a few notes about it?"

"Oh, ma'am, it isn't all that important. I don't want to take up any more of your time. Just wanted to get the story off my chest."

"No, please. I've got plenty of time and I'd like to make a record of this."

As they left, Jane emerged from her hiding place, smiling.

She'd thought of a pea museum as sort of a campy joke, but here was proof that even peas could be important to someone. Lifesaving to a whole family, even. She was glad to have eavesdropped on such a pleasant conversation. And glad, too, that the old gentleman had accidentally picked someone as kind and patient as Sharlene to tell his story to. She wondered if the board of directors realized what an asset Sharlene really was and resolved to share that view with anyone who would listen.

Jane completed her tour of the room and was heading for Sharlene's office when she passed the main door. Shelley was just coming in. "Remind me to tell you about a conversation I overheard," Jane said.

"Something to do with Ms. Palmer's death?"

"Oh, no. Just a very nice, heartwarming story." She lowered her voice. "This must be the old man who told it."

Sharlene was ushering him out a door labeled STAFF ONLY. He was loaded down with pea-museum memorabilia, including a pile of T-shirts for his grandchildren, and he was still trying to pay for it, an offer Sharlene wouldn't hear of.

When he'd gone, she turned to Jane and Shelley. Today she was wearing a proper black suit with a creamy white blouse. Her wild red hair was somewhat confined by a black velvet ribbon. She looked extremely professional.

She said, "I guess you know we're in kind of a mess today, but it shouldn't keep you from working. Thanks again for coming."

"Let's get on with it, then," Shelley said. "The same room I was in last week?"

"Yes, the boardroom."

They entered the STAFF ONLY door and Jane found herself

in a rabbit warren of offices almost as cluttered and interesting as the museum itself. She could suddenly understand the desire to have a new facility. It would be maddening to have to work around such clutter, no matter how well organized it was. The boardroom was the least crowded spot, but even it had things stored and stacked in cartons.

"I can bring Jane up to speed, Sharlene," Shelley said. "Now, Jane, here's the computer."

As Sharlene departed, Jane said warily, "Why are you telling me this?"

"Because you know how to operate a computer."

"Shelley, all I have is a little PC with a word-processing program, a checkbook program, and a bunch of games. I don't know anything about—"

"You'll figure it out. It's just a matter of transferring data from a written sheet to the database—"

"Database," Jane groaned.

"—and assigning a number. Here's what we do: each item in the museum will be assigned an identification number—there's a sheet Ms. Palmer drew up explaining how to determine the number. Then each item has a description—what it is, approximate date, how and when it was acquired if anyone knows, value if known."

"Shelley!" Jane exclaimed. "How would *we* know any of these things?"

"In a lot of cases, some of the information is on the display itself. Don't worry. We don't have to guess or research much. Other, much more knowledgeable people will be filling in the blanks later. We're just doing the initial scut work, which is to assign the numbers, put in what information we can get easily, and label the item with the assigned number.

We do that with these special little tags that won't harm the exhibit items. They're very expensive, so don't waste them."

"I'm in way over my head," Jane said. "Why have you done this to me?"

"You are Woman! You can manage," Shelley ordered.

Out of the corner of her eye Jane caught a glimpse of a cat curled up on top of a stack of boxes. She reached out to bestow a comforting pat and immediately jerked her hand back. "Oh, my God! Shelley! That cat's dead!"

"Of course it's dead. It's stuffed."

"Why is there a stuffed cat in here?" Jane's voice had risen to an almost hysterical pitch.

Sharlene had come back in the room with a handful of paperwork. "Oh, that's Mr. Auguste Snellen's mother cat. Heidi."

"That statement appears to make sense to you," Jane said.

Sharlene laughed. "A long time ago, all the peas for sale were kept in one big warehouse and it got a horrible rat infestation. The people who worked for him wanted to have the rats poisoned, but Mr. Snellen didn't like poisons. And he didn't like what they were going to cost, either, and said he wasn't going to have a warehouse full of peas and dead rats. So he went out and got this cat. She was pregnant, see. And after she had her kittens, she taught them all how to kill rats and the problem was solved. Mr. Snellen made a pet of her and said she'd saved his business. He was awfully fond of her. Even had a picture taken with her—when she was still alive, of course—and I keep a copy on my desk."

"You have a picture of Auguste Snellen on your desk?" Jane asked.

"Well, it's silly, I know. He died ages before I was even

born, but I sort of felt like I knew him. And he looks like such a nice old thing."

"I think that's wonderful," Jane said.

"I'll show it to you later," Sharlene offered. "Anyway, when the cat died, they say Mr. Snellen was heartbroken. She used to curl up on his desk while he was working, so he had her stuffed so she could stay on his desk. She's held up pretty well, considering."

Jane looked at the cat closer. It was an orange cat, curled in a tidy ball, head on front paws, with green marble eyes and a few mangy-looking bald spots. But some long-gone taxidermist had done a good job of making her look natural.

Jane suddenly laughed. "Well, I hope when I'm through here, people can say the same of me. 'She's held up pretty well, considering.' Let's get to work, Shelley."

Chapter**7**

Jane was enormously relieved to discover that the job wasn't nearly as hard as it had sounded. Regina Palmer's instructions on how to assign the item numbers were clear and easy to understand and appeared to account for every possible contingency in a marvelously logical manner. Even the computer was cooperative. The database was one specifically designed for museum inventories and was easy to use. Shelley had spent time the week before recording many of the items on paper forms that exactly duplicated the computer program's format, so all Jane had to do was assign the number and enter the information. Once she stopped worrying about the information that was missing, it was really a snap.

Among the many stacked items in the boardroom was an old radio in working condition. Jane found an "oldies" AM station and spent two hours happily listening to the Everly Brothers, Elvis, and the Supremes while typing information into the computer. When Shelley and Lisa Quigley came into the boardroom and announced that it was lunchtime, she was surprised. Shelley had spent her time in the farm-implement room, filling out more forms, which she set down next to the computer.

Lisa Quigley said, "There are snack machines here, but I wouldn't advise eating from them. There's also a little strip mall next door that has a few fast-food restaurants that are pretty good. Pizza, burgers, salad, and pasta. I'd recommend the salad shop. What are your preferences? I'll go get us all something."

"No, sit down. I'll go," Shelley insisted. She took their orders and disappeared.

Jane turned off the radio, shut down the computer, and stood and stretched.

"We really appreciate your help," Lisa said, glancing through the stack of papers Shelley had left on the table.

"It's actually fun," Jane said. "I'm curious to see some of the things I've been entering. I can't imagine what a 'circa 1870 crank-handled pea shucker' looks like."

Lisa smiled and sat down at the long table in the center of the room. Jane took a chair across from her. When Jane had first met Lisa and she'd given them their instructions for the reenactment, she'd looked like a trim, contented thirty-five-year-old. Now she looked haggard, unhappy, and a decade older.

"I'm terribly sorry about Ms. Palmer's death," Jane said. "It must be a tremendous loss to all of you."

Lisa nodded. "She was so important in so many ways. Especially to me. She was my best friend."

"I'm sorry. I didn't know," Jane said. "You've known her for a long time, then?"

"Ever since college. We were taking a history course and discovered that we were both doing papers on the identical subject—'Women's Roles in the Agrarian Society of Pre-Renaissance France.' It was kind of spooky. Instead of competing for the documents we both needed, we got permission from the professor to do the paper jointly. It was marvelous working with Regina. She had a real gift for language."

"I know. Her instructions on cataloging are very clear," Jane said. "But surely you brought something to the paper as well."

"Oh, I'm dogged. I never let a piece of research go until I've squeezed everything out of it," Lisa said with a self-deprecating smile. "We were a good combination. Got an A on the paper. Had it published in an academic journal. And became friends, too. We could have made names for ourselves in scholastic circles, I think. But we both badly wanted to get out into the real world."

"And so you both came here to the Snellen?"

"Regina came first. She was a year ahead of me in school. I'd taken a year to work and pay off some student loans halfway through. Regina figured out the long-term plan—she wanted to find a small museum, otherwise we'd have come in at the very lowest level and had to spend years, if not decades, working our way up. The Snellen was perfect. Regina fell in love with this place the minute she walked in the door, she said. And she interviewed with Miss Snellen and they got on together awfully well. The Snellen had a director who was retiring and Miss Snellen wanted somebody young and enthusiastic and bright who could see a future for the museum instead of just going along the way it was forever. I suppose Miss Snellen had in mind then that she might leave most of her fortune to the museum, but she didn't even hint at that. Anyway, Regina took the job."

Lisa had been looking at the wall behind Jane as she spoke and suddenly recalled herself. "I'm sorry. This must be awfully boring to you."

"Not at all. I'm fascinated," Jane said. It wasn't quite the truth, but she sensed that Lisa needed to talk, and she was more than willing to listen if it would help assuage her grief. "What happened next?"

"Regina took over the directorship, found an apartment, and got to work. She'd only been here about a month or two before she figured out her long-term plans. She called and explained to me some of what she had in mind—more involvement in the Pea Festival, renovations in the budget structure, and such. But she said the one thing the museum desperately needed was a good public-relations and promotion plan. And she wanted me to do that. I was ready to enroll for my last semester, but I dropped all my courses and signed up instead for advertising classes. Whole new world to me!"

"It must have been," Jane said. That helped explain why Lisa hadn't seemed to fit the stereotypical mold of the aggressive, outgoing publicity person. She was basically a scholarly type who'd taken up promotion for purely practical reasons.

"It would have been the most hideous semester of my life, except that I had so much to look forward to. Regina convinced Miss Snellen that although I didn't have much training in promotion, I knew history and was a hard worker. Miss Snellen agreed to give me a chance—well, after all, qualifications didn't mean so much then. The former director had been a retired high-school science teacher. So I came here. Regina found a bigger apartment so that we could live together and work on museum concerns in the evenings without having to cart paperwork back and forth."

"You're smiling as if that was fun, to work day and night," Jane said.

"It *was* fun, really. The challenge of it. The Snellen Museum was like a lump of clay just waiting to be formed into something. When I came here, it was only open three afternoons a week, and as often as not, the only volunteer guide we had was Miss Snellen herself. But Regina solicited some women's clubs to sponsor volunteer guides. I trained them and then we opened the museum six days a week, charging a small admissions fee to help with the finances. Regina and I began visiting local schools, hauling along exhibits and encouraging teachers to bring classes here. Meanwhile, Regina hired Sharlene, who took over a lot of the paperwork, and that allowed Regina and me to finally start spiffing up the exhibits themselves."

"What a huge amount of work!" Jane said.

"Yes, and sometimes it seemed to go so slowly. But almost always in the right direction. Of course, there was one summer that the city was putting in a new sewer line and the street was closed. I think we had about fourteen hearty souls the whole season who went to the trouble of climbing through the construction rubble to get here."

"How discouraging!"

"Yes, but Miss Snellen was wonderful. When she realized that the museum really could be an attraction, not just a personal hobby of hers, she got behind us with the funding.

She even manned the gift shop a day a week, though standing for long periods was hard for her. She encouraged Regina to write articles for various publications that would make the Snellen, if not a household name, at least a name that a few history buffs had heard of. I remember the first time somebody actually came from out of town specifically to visit the museum. We were so excited that we nearly buried the guy in attention."

Lisa paused and looked away as Shelley came in with their lunches, and said, almost under her breath, "There were good times."

The longing in her tone broke Jane's heart. "There will be lots more good times," she said. "Just think how exciting it'll be when the new museum starts taking shape and when you are moving things."

"Yes, you're right," Lisa said with a sigh. "But Regina won't be here to see it."

"But she'll be with all of you in spirit," Jane said, cringing inwardly at the cliché but unable to think of anything else comforting to say.

Shelley set out their food, distributed napkins and plastic forks, and said, "Who will be in charge now? Will you become director, Lisa?"

"Oh, no! I hope not. It wouldn't suit me at all. I've come to really like my job and I do it well, I think. There's a lot of really boring detail work that goes with the directorship that I'd hate. Correspondence and bookkeeping."

"I guess that's why you have an assistant director, to step in if necessary," Shelley said. "Will Derek Delano be given the position, do you think?"

Lisa didn't answer right away. Then she said cautiously, "I suppose he might."

"I hope he isn't," Shelley said frankly. She drizzled dressing over her salad.

"Why is that?" Lisa asked.

Shelley looked up at her. "Because he's obnoxious."

"Well . . ." Lisa began.

"Look," Shelley said, "I realize you have to work with him and I'm not trying to jeopardize your professional relationship, but that man's a jerk and you must know it. Were you in the trailer yesterday when I returned that box of gift-shop stuff and he called me 'babe'? That's just not the way to treat a woman you don't know, and a volunteer at that. If the museum put him in charge, they'd have a sexual harassment suit on their hands in a week."

Lisa looked stunned at Shelley's bluntness, but acknowledged her remarks with a nod. "I'm afraid you're right. And I know Regina would have agreed."

"Why? Did he try that stuff on her, too? His own boss?" Jane asked.

"Yes, 'tried.' But it was so blatant—" Lisa hesitated again.

Shelley was on a roll and wouldn't let it go at that. "What was so blatant?"

"Well, he was after her job. Everybody knew that. He didn't even bother to disguise it. He was always mentioning how she'd be moving on to bigger and better museums once the Snellen was in its new building and she'd made her name in the profession. At first he flirted with her, which was really inappropriate. Then, when she rejected his requests for dates, he got sulky, and when she became involved with Whitney, he started making remarks that skated awfully close to being sexual innuendos. I'm sure Derek thought Regina found him attractive in spite of all the evidence to the contrary and would push the board to appoint him in her place when she left."

"So she *was* leaving the museum?" Jane asked.

"No, she wasn't. I was saying what Derek thought. He was wrong, but nothing could convince him of it."

"I don't get it," Shelley said. "If she was his boss and he was so obnoxious, why didn't she fire him? Or explain it to the board of directors, if they're the ones who do the firing?"

"Pride," Lisa answered. "That's all. Regina could be awfully stiff-necked at times. She'd searched high and low for an assistant, interviewed a mob of candidates. Somehow Derek managed to behave in the interviews and she recommended him to the board. She just couldn't bring herself to admit to them that she'd made a mistake. And it might have actually been hard to get rid of him. He's superbly well qualified, academically. More so than either Regina or I when we came here."

Jane nibbled at her salad, reflecting that it was interesting how Shelley's bluntness often encouraged people to talk about things they'd never normally say, especially to strangers. Lisa Quigley hardly knew them, yet Shelley had her "talking shop" in minutes. Of course, part of it was probably the fact that poor Lisa had unexpectedly lost a good friend as well as a co-worker.

"Don't you suppose the board knows what he's like?" Jane asked. "Babs McDonald strikes me as a sharp woman."

Lisa kept poking at her salad as if she really wanted to eat but couldn't quite bring herself to it. "Yes, Babs must realize. And I imagine Regina talked to Jumper about it. She depended a lot on his judgment."

"Then it doesn't sound like there's too much danger of Derek being appointed director," Shelley said. "Who else is on the board?"

"Jumper, Babs, Georgia Snellen—do you know her?"

"We do," Shelley said curtly. "We saw her at the Festival. With Derek."

Lisa looked for a minute like she was going to question Shelley, but went on instead. "Then there's an accountant Jumper recommended a few years ago when Miss Snellen died and we suddenly had a large endowment. He's in Alaska right now, visiting his brother who's a park ranger or something."

"Is that all?" Jane asked.

"No, there's a history professor from the local junior college, but he's traveling in Europe this summer, doing research for a paper. Then there are a half-dozen honorary board members. They aren't voting directors, but they're community leaders whose support is important, and their opinions are pretty highly valued."

"So right now, the appointment of a new director lies with Jumper, Babs, and Georgia."

"Only Jumper and Georgia, theoretically. Babs is the president of the board and votes only in case of a tie."

"Let me guess," Shelley said. "Jumper would probably vote against Derek's appointment. Georgia would probably vote for it. And Babs would break the tie."

Lisa thought for a moment. "Yes, but . . . I think parliamentary procedure *allows* the president to break a tie, but doesn't *require* it. So Babs might refuse to cast the deciding vote and make everybody wait until the other two board members return or can be reached to cast a vote by mail. I imagine they'll just appoint him acting director while they search for a new person entirely. Unless—"

The word hung in the air for a moment until Jane asked, "Unless what?"

"Unless Derek's arrested for murdering Regina," Lisa said.

Chapter**8**

"**Do you think** he killed her?" Shelley asked quietly.

Lisa seemed to suddenly realize that she'd gone too far. "No, no. Not at all. I shouldn't have even thought that, much less said it. I'm really sorry."

Shelley brushed aside her objections. "It's natural to wonder when something so terrible happens to someone you love. Do you believe the shooting was deliberate?"

"It had to be, didn't it?" Lisa said, her voice catching. "The police said the gun came from the museum. That had to be deliberate, stealing the gun. And it's hard to imagine why anybody would take it on purpose, then shoot someone with it by accident."

"Who could have taken it?"

Lisa shrugged helplessly. "Anybody, I guess. Well, anybody who knows where the keys to the cases are kept, and that's anyone who's ever worked here. Regina was awfully trusting of everyone and wasn't concerned with theft. In fact, the board had to overrule her objections to updating and improving the security system."

"I suppose the police fingerprinted the display case," Jane said.

"I guess they must have," Lisa said. "But they might have found a ton of prints or none at all. The kids who come here love that display. They all lean on it and touch it. Besides, we had a leak from the sink in the upstairs rest room last week that made a big stain on the wall behind the case. We had to wrestle it out into the middle of the room. It took half the staff to move it out, then move it back when the painting was finished. And in the meantime, it was in the traffic path, and I imagine many people who visited the room touched the display as they squeezed past. But if the— the person who did this awful thing had any sense at all, he cleaned off all the prints."

"And you think that person was Derek Delano?" Shelley asked.

"No. No, I really don't." Lisa obviously regretted her earlier remark about him. She put down her fork and fiddled around pulling her hair back and reclipping a tortoiseshell barrette while she thought. Finally she said, "Derek is ambitious and nasty and has an ego the size of Texas, but I don't think he's truly mean-spirited. And he's very bright and well educated. I believe if it *had* gotten through to him that he probably wasn't ever going to be director of the Snellen, he'd have just altered his plan and gone somewhere else to move his career along. I don't think he especially liked or disliked Regina, either. I'm not sure he *can* like or dislike people. I think he categorizes them as useful or not useful."

"And Georgia Snellen is useful?" Shelley asked.

"Oh, you've seen her hanging on him? I guess either she's convinced him she is or—well, to be vulgar—she's useful, and handy, in other ways."

Jane had been working her way through her salad, which was very good, while Shelley and Lisa talked. Now she closed the clear plastic container and started tidying up the table. "Was there anyone who did dislike Ms. Palmer?" she asked.

"Well, Caspar Snellen never bothered to disguise his feelings, but other than that, I don't know. Anybody else who found fault with her would be unlikely to tell me about it."

"And why did Caspar Snellen dislike her?" Jane asked.

"Money. His aunt's money, which he counted on getting and didn't. And the fact that he's a miserable person who goes around imagining that everybody's conspiring against him." Lisa shuddered a little and suddenly said, "I really appreciate you two letting me blow off steam. I'm sorry—I probably ruined your lunch and said a lot of dumb things I shouldn't have."

"Not in the least," Jane assured her.

"You know, I've realized since Saturday that when someone close to you dies, people tend to think the kind, polite thing to do is try to take your mind off it. As if it's somehow ghoulish or tasteless to even mention the person's name in polite company."

"It's well meant," Shelley said.

"I know. But it can make you feel that everybody just wants to forget they existed at all. Thanks again for listening. It helps. And thanks for picking up lunch, Shelley. I think this is the first time in days that I just sat down for this long. Oh, give me your receipt and I'll make sure Sharlene reimburses you."

When Lisa had gone, Jane gave the stuffed cat a preoccupied pet and went right back to work so she could push away the thought that was troubling her. To lose a best friend must be an awful thing. If Shelley were suddenly taken out of her life, Jane couldn't imagine how she'd cope. Nobody could fill that empty space. And it must be worse for Lisa Quigley, who had no husband or children and, given her work schedule, probably no other close friends.

Jane forced herself to concentrate on cataloging a collection of turn-of-the-century corsets and petticoats.

By two-thirty, Jane was more than ready for a break. She used her computer a lot at home: she'd been working—or rather playing—at a story that she hoped would someday miraculously turn into a novel. But at home she was always up and down, throwing in a load of laundry, letting the dog in and out of the backyard, running errands. She seldom sat in front of the screen for such long, intense periods. And the strain was getting to her neck and eyes. She moved over to the board table, sat down, gingerly rested her heels on the very edge of the table, and slouched into the chair. The change in posture hurt, but in a good, stretchy way.

When the door opened, she hastily sat up.

"Taking a break?" Babs McDonald said. "Put your feet back up. You can't do that table any harm. I did a little nursing during World War Two and the head nurse always told us that if we put our feet up every single chance we got, we'd add at least five years to our lives. You're Jane, right?"

"Jane Jeffry, yes."

"I'm Babs McDonald. I hope everybody's fawned over you and your friend Shelley for helping us out. We're really enormously grateful."

"Everybody's fawned very nicely," Jane said with a smile. "And I'm finding it very interesting. Besides, it gets me out of the house and away from my children for a while. By August, that's a real perk."

"Oh, yes. Summer vacation." Babs had brought along a cup of coffee and sat down to put a packet of powdered dairy mix into it. "I remember when Daisy was raising Caspar and Georgia. By the end of vacation, she was exhausted."

"Daisy Snellen, you mean? She raised—?" Jane was confused.

"Not officially, of course, but her brother was—not to speak ill of the dead—but he was a bum. His wife left him and the kids and he pretty much dumped them on poor Daisy. I helped her out as much as I could, but I'm not one of those women with a maternal pilot light that makes me automatically love children. Even very nice children. And Caspar and Georgia weren't ever especially nice children. You've probably met them and could have guessed that."

She was stirring in the dairy mix and looking at the result with disgust. Jane was again struck by how well Babs seemed to "fit" her age. Her thick white hair was in a Gibson Girl type of loose knot on top of her head today. She wore crisply tailored white slacks, an obviously expensive light blue safari-style blouse, and a gorgeous fuchsia, navy, and white silk scarf tied as a belt. She looked both stylish and comfortable, as if it came naturally.

WAR AND PEAS

"I've only seen Caspar Snellen once—no, twice, including this morning—and the first time he was very rude."

"Oh, he's his father all over again. But how his father got to be that way is a mystery to me. Old Auguste Snellen was about the kindest, most courteous old gentleman I ever met and his wife was a sweet little dumpling of a woman. And Daisy's parents were lovely people, too, but they died very young. Her brother, who was the father of Caspar and Georgia, was only a teenager when Auguste died, and Daisy was about twenty. Auguste left his fortune to Daisy, supposedly because his grandson was so young. But I think old Auguste had already seen the writing on the wall and knew the boy was going to turn out badly."

"You knew Auguste Snellen? I thought he was born way back in the 1850s."

"Yes, he was. But he lived to be eighty years old. He died in 1935, I think. I was only fifteen then, but I thought he was a dear old man. Sharlene feels the same about him, and all she's ever known is his picture. Daisy always said that as a grandfather, employer, and friend, he was lovely, but as a businessman, he was tough, independent, and rather secretive. He did all his own bookkeeping because he didn't want an accountant to know his business." She paused, then asked, "What did you mean about seeing Caspar this morning?"

Shelley slipped quietly into the room and smiled at Babs as she laid a fresh set of forms on the stack Jane was working from.

"I was taking a little tour of the museum before Shelley arrived. I saw him standing in the doorway of that big room just to the left of the entry."

"What was he doing?"

"Looking around for someone or something. He ignored me," Jane said.

"Best way to handle him. I never liked the way he's always hanging around here like it's a boarding house. And I like it less now."

"Why now?"

Babs cocked an expressive white eyebrow. "Why do you suppose, dear? Because in all likelihood, he killed Regina."

There was none of Lisa's lost-in-grief-and-don't-know-what-I'm-saying tone to this remark. Babs was simply saying what she thought, as she was apparently used to doing.

"Oh, my dears! Don't look so horrified," Babs said. "I don't mean he necessarily murdered her—not on purpose. Caspar is a bully and a threatener. I can well imagine him stealing that gun and thinking what power it might give him, however temporary, to wave it around at Regina, or maybe even shoot it at her, meaning to frighten the daylights out of her, but miss. And then, when he stupidly hit her by mistake—"

"Have you told the police this?" Jane asked.

"Of course I have. Can't let the fool get away with it. He's done enough damage in his life without being allowed free rein to do more. When I think of how he broke poor Daisy's heart—"

"What did he do to her?" Shelley asked.

"Oh, a hundred vicious, petty things, but two years before her death, he did the worst. He and Georgia got themselves into some kind of crooked investment scheme that blew up in their faces. They had to pay up or face going to jail. And, of course, they couldn't pay off without going to Daisy for the money. She was thoroughly disgusted with both of them by then. Naturally she wouldn't let Snellens go to jail and besmirch the family name, but she really put them through hoops before she wrote out the checks. Shortly after that, in retaliation, Caspar managed to insinuate one of his disreputable friends into her house—a young woman who acted as secretary and nurse, but was really spying on Daisy. After a few months of accumulating information and making up stories, Caspar tried to have Daisy declared incompetent."

"But he didn't succeed." Jane had never even met Daisy Snellen, but was appalled nevertheless.

"Of course not. Jumper, who was already working for Daisy, really did a number on him. Let him get clear into a court hearing and showed Caspar up as a greedy fool. Not that it was hard. Caspar's so stupid, really. I'm trying to remember some of the things . . ."

She frowned into the now scummy, cold coffee cup and suddenly grinned. "Oh, yes. My favorite! Caspar's stooge took a photo of Daisy with her hair tied up in rags. Now, I'll admit a woman who curls her hair that old-fashioned way looks pretty crazy—like those medieval monarchs who went mad and stuck straws in their hair. Wild bits sticking out every which way, you know. But when Caspar's sleazy attorney produced this picture with a flourish, Jumper calmly supplied a copy of a ladies' magazine from the 1920s that Regina had found that illustrated how to tie up your hair in rags. And, by sheer good luck, the judge said he remembered his own grandmother looking like that every Saturday night so she'd have curly hair for church on Sunday."

Babs laughed like a schoolgirl for a second, then turned

serious again. "Daisy treasured the memory of that moment, but was humiliated by the whole experience. Humiliated and deeply hurt."

"She must have been," Jane said. "How awful for her. Where was Georgia during all this incompetency thing?"

"Hiding. Trying to pretend she knew nothing about it so she could ally herself with whoever won. That evening, after the judge had thrown Caspar out of court and given him a verbal drubbing, Georgia turned up with flowers and candy to congratulate Daisy—as if Daisy really *were* too dotty to notice what Georgia was about. Her behavior really made Daisy even more angry."

Babs got up and poured the coffee into the little sink in a corner of the room, rinsed out the cup, and tossed it in the trash. "After that," she said as she came back to the table, "Daisy changed her will. Originally she'd left a third to the museum and a third each to Caspar and Georgia. She altered it to give each of them a million dollars, which she felt was generous enough to satisfy her obligation to the Snellen name, and the rest to the museum. She said, and I believe she was quite right, that they were going to come to bad ends anyway, and the more money they had, the sooner it would happen. So Caspar—who's never been able to admit that he was at fault for anything—decided that Regina had 'conned' Daisy into rewriting the will. He's spent the last two years getting one ambulance chaser after another to contest the will. I imagine he's already gone through all the money he did receive and—"

The door opened rather suddenly and a biker strode into the room.

Shelley and Jane drew back in alarm. The man had on a

tie-dyed T-shirt under a black leather jacket festooned with chains. He wore a bandanna with a flame design low on his forehead. Reflecting sunglasses, black leather pants, and thigh-high boots almost completed his look.

He also carried a briefcase.

"Jumper!" Babs exclaimed. "I thought you'd forgotten the meeting!"

Chapter**9**

Since Babs found nothing strange about Jumper Cable's appearance, Jane and Shelley didn't comment, either. Jumper took off the shades and jacket, sat down at the table after greeting them affably, and started removing papers from the beat-up brown briefcase.

"Are you having a meeting here?" Jane asked. "Do you want us to leave?"

"Board meetings are open to the public," Babs said, but she sounded hesitant.

"No, no. We'll go fill some of the forms instead," Jane said. "We have plenty to do elsewhere."

Jumper and Babs looked relieved.

Shelley gave Jane a bunch of blank forms and a pencil and they left the boardroom. "Where shall we start?" Jane asked.

"I've been working in a room on the second floor, but—"

"Isn't there somewhere more private where we could make ourselves useful?" Jane asked.

WAR AND PEAS

"Exactly my thought," Shelley said. "Let's look over the Dreaded Basement."

It was the basement nightmares are made of—huge, with stone walls, a dank, musty smell, and a labyrinth of boxes, furniture, mysterious equipment, snaky old wiring, and a concrete floor. It was, however, as clean as such a place could be. A push broom with bristles worn down like an old man's teeth stood at the ready by the door. Though it was a single room with support pillars, the stored furniture and boxes created head-high rooms and hallways.

"Do you suppose anyone's down here besides us?" Jane asked.

"There was a light on when we came in. Let's look," Shelley replied.

They prowled the basement, finding an amazing variety of things, but no people—if you didn't consider a family grouping of very badly constructed mannequins that appeared to be posed for eating a meal over a table that had long since disappeared. Jane had rounded a corner and come upon them unexpectedly and nearly had a heart attack at the sight of the black-suited father frozen in the act of carving a missing roast with a wicked-looking knife. She yelped with surprise and Shelley came running.

"My God!" Shelley exclaimed. "He looks just like my dentist."

"Are we going to have to categorize all this stuff?" Jane asked.

"I hope not. I'm certain they won't want to take along something like the Happy Family here. Although"—she grinned wickedly—"I do wonder how you go about disposing of something like them."

"Mike might like to take the daughter to college with him. She's kinda cute," Jane said.

"And you could stand Mother at your kitchen sink so that anybody glancing in the window might imagine somebody domestic lived at your house."

"What's this?" Jane went over to look at a large piece of furniture against the wall. It was eight feet tall and nearly as wide and was composed entirely of wooden drawers about nine inches square. At the front of each drawer was a small brass "picture frame" with a card slipped into it. The cards had numbers and letters on them, like "A34 x N47." Jane cautiously opened a drawer. It was full of shriveled-up peas.

"This must have been Auguste Snellen's storage for his pea experiments, don't you think?" Shelley said.

"I wonder if any of them would grow if you planted them."

"Probably not. Well, maybe so, come to think of it. Didn't they find a bunch of wheat in a pyramid that they got to sprout after five thousand years or something? I saw a program about it on television once."

"Wonder what the numbers mean," Jane said. "Maybe a cross between two other kinds. See, up there at the top are a bunch of drawers without the 'x something' part."

"He probably had all the details recorded in books somewhere," Shelley said. "Some of the cards in the little frames look much older and more faded than others. There were probably lots of duds that got disposed of—"

"Oh! The Depression pea story. I almost forgot to tell you," Jane said. She related the conversation she'd overheard when she first arrived at the museum.

WAR AND PEAS

"That is nice," Shelley said when Jane was done. "It really sums up an era, doesn't it? All the kids out crawling around the field to pick the peas so they'd have ground cover to hold the soil down the next year. We couldn't get *our* kids to do that."

"I bet we could if it was a matter of eating or starving."

"How nice that it was Sharlene he picked to tell the story to," Shelley said.

"Just what I thought. Shelley . . ." She paused for a moment. "It really isn't any of our business who killed Regina, is it?"

"No, it isn't. But . . ."

Jane sat down on a wooden crate and spoke quietly. "I was determined not to get involved. Not to care about someone I never knew. But now that I've come to know some of these people, I find that I'm caring in spite of myself."

"Me, too," Shelley admitted. She perched on the corner of a sturdy buffet table. "Mel would wash our mouths out with soap if he heard us. We've gotten to know and like people who *did* care for Regina. I guess that's what makes the difference. I feel so sorry for Sharlene and Lisa, losing someone they thought so much of in their different ways."

"But not Babs? You don't feel sorry for her?"

"I don't think anybody'd ever dare feel sorry for her. Besides, she really didn't say anything much about her relationship with Regina. I wonder if she even liked her."

"Good question," Jane said. "She must have respected her, though. She's the president of the board of directors. If she hadn't thought Regina was good at her job, she could probably have had her fired."

"Yes, if she were incompetent," Shelley agreed. "But I

have the feeling that Babs is the kind of person who could despise someone personally and still recognize their good traits."

"You know what I'm wondering?" Jane said. "Whether whoever shot her meant to."

"You means Babs's theory that Caspar Snellen did it by accident?"

"No, what I really meant was this: it was a well-staged riot. The reenactors knew what they were doing, but nobody else did. Couldn't someone have been trying to shoot someone else and Regina ran in front of the target?"

Shelley considered for a moment. "I guess that's possible. Meaning that Derek and Caspar, who are by far the best suspects, might have been the intended victims instead?"

"Or anybody else, for that matter. Neither of them was in the reenactment, though, were they? I saw Jumper in his farm-boy clothes, but I don't remember the other two."

"I don't believe they were participants," Shelley said. "But anybody could have been lurking in those woods. It's pretty overgrown very near where we were walking."

"But if they were in the woods, that puts them back at being suspects, not victims, doesn't it?"

"Right. It does."

"I couldn't sleep last night," Jane said, "for thinking about it. I've tried and tried to picture where everyone was, but I just can't bring it into focus. I was only thinking about myself. I really was about ninety percent convinced it was really happening. Somehow I don't think the shooting was an accident, though. Just my gut reaction."

"You're probably right," Shelley agreed. "But think about it . . . from what we've heard, Regina seemed to be a sort of ordinary person. A bit dull, perhaps. Ambitious enough, but not a hint of trampling ambition. A good friend to Lisa, a good employer to Sharlene, and a good enough employee, apparently, as far as Babs is concerned. Not the sort of person to inspire passionate emotions. Not passionate enough to lead to murder."

"Yes, but there's a lot of money involved," Jane said. "Millions. That could certainly inspire passion in some people. Like Caspar Snellen. And possibly that awful Georgia, his sister. Just because she was canny enough not to be overt about her resentment doesn't mean she wasn't just as greedy as Caspar."

"Right. But killing Regina wouldn't have made any difference," Shelley said. "She wasn't the one who inherited the money. The museum was. And I don't imagine her death will change that. Certainly not now. Probably not even if she'd died sooner. Miss Snellen left her fortune to the museum. Granted, she had every reason to believe a woman as young as Regina would continue as director, but still ..."

Jane nodded. "But if it was Caspar or Georgia, it might have been just sheer frustration that they weren't able to change the will. Or maybe they imagine that Georgia could divert some of the money to the two of them if Regina was out of the way."

"What do you mean?"

"I'm not sure." Jane thought for a moment. "Okay. What if Georgia thought that without Regina in the way, her toy boy Derek would be director and, as a member of the board, she could get his salary kicked way up and get her hands on part of it herself?"

Shelley shook her head. "Not with Babs McDonald and

an accountant on the board. Don't you imagine the board keeps a close eye on the finances?"

"Mmm. Bad example, I guess. What if it's not the money at all?"

"What else?"

"Well, we were talking about passion. Regina was engaged, you know. And we've never even laid eyes on this Whitney guy. Surely an engagement involves some degree of passion. And didn't Sharlene say the engagement had been an on-and-off sort of thing? It might have been a rather tumultuous relationship."

"You might have a point," Shelley said. "Isn't it odd that nobody's said much about him? Everybody here must have known Whitney. He's the architect of the new building. He must have attended board meetings, surveyed this building pretty thoroughly, and so forth."

"That *is* strange, now that you mention it. It's as if he hasn't made an impression of any kind."

Shelley stood up. "We'd better get on with something more productive than this, Jane. I hardly know where to start down here. Let me think about it overnight. Let's go back up and finish the room I was almost done with." She picked up her clipboard and Jane grabbed a book to serve as one.

"Jane? Shelley?" a faint voice called from the doorway.

They wound their way back through the artificial hallways of stored items and found Sharlene standing at the doorway, shading her eyes against the bare light bulb overhead.

"What's up, Sharlene?" Jane asked.

"How long have you been down here?" Sharlene replied.

Jane glanced at her watch. "About an hour. Why?"

"You didn't come upstairs during the board meeting?"

"No. Why do you ask?"

"I was hoping you'd seen something. Oh, this is so awful. Somebody's been in Ms. Palmer's office, rummaging through things like mad."

"During the board meeting, you mean?" Jane asked.

"I think so."

"Then you know at least a couple of people that it wasn't," Shelley said briskly.

"Well, not really. Babs went out to get some financial statements from the files. Tom went to the bathroom. Georgia left to make a phone call—"

"Wait," Jane said. "Start at the beginning. How do you know this happened during the board meeting?"

Sharlene thought for a minute. "I guess I really don't. I went into her office this morning, to put some flowers on her desk. I guess it was stupid, but I saw them for sale on a street corner on the way to work and it seemed a nice thing—"

"It was nice," Shelley said. "You don't have to explain yourself on that score. But what time was that?"

"Nine or so."

"And did you lock the door when you came out?" Jane asked.

"I think so. Yes. Well, maybe."

"So anybody might have gone in there anytime today?"

"Not really. There are always people in the staff area— the tour guides on their breaks and such. Somebody would have seen if anyone else went inside."

"Wasn't that true during the board meeting, too?" Shelley asked.

Sharlene shook her head. "I don't think so. There weren't any scheduled tours this afternoon and there were only the two volunteers and they were sitting out in the lobby the whole time, chatting with the woman who was working the gift shop. I already asked them."

"Was anything taken from the office?" Jane asked.

"I don't know. It's such a mess," Sharlene said. "It'll take me forever to straighten it out. I better start—"

"No," Jane said. "Let's go up and get the room locked right now and call the police."

"The police! Why?" She stared at Jane for a minute, then added, "Oh, of course. How dumb of me."

Chapter 10

Fortunately, Babs McDonald had known about the vandalism sooner and thought faster. By the time Shelley, Jane, and Sharlene emerged from the basement, Babs had locked up Regina's office and phoned Mel. She'd also corralled everyone from the board meeting back into the boardroom and shooed the three of them in as well before taking a chair from which she could keep an eye on the violated office through the open door.

"That nice young man who's a friend of yours was on his way over anyway," Babs said to Jane. "I don't believe either of you has met Mr. Abbot, have you? Whitney Abbot, our architect. This is Jane Jeffry and Shelley Nowack. They're doing the preliminary data entry on the museum contents."

Jane's first impression of him was of cool perfection. Perfect teeth, perfectly groomed John Kennedy hair, a perfectly fitted charcoal-gray, three-piece suit without a wrinkle or a speck of lint (or cat hair, which any dark garment Jane owned was sure to be blighted by) anywhere. He wasn't a big man and probably hadn't stood more than an inch or two taller than Regina, but he looked fit in an expensive handball-and-sauna way.

He shook their hands—Jane noticed his fingernails were immaculate and manicured to a subtle gloss—and said, "That's a big job. We're all grateful." He spoke quite formally.

"Ms. Palmer's plan makes it much easier than it might otherwise have been," Shelley said, matching his formality. "We didn't know her, but we're very sorry about her death. It was terrible for everyone and, I'm sure, especially so for you."

He nodded. "An unimaginable loss."

The remark wasn't so much cold as it was meaningless, Jane thought. But then, they were strangers to him. Why should he pour out his heart? Perhaps he was still in a state of shock. Or perhaps he was just a very reserved person who was unaccustomed to expressing his feelings freely.

There was a moment's awkward silence before the entire group turned at the sound of Caspar Snellen's voice in the doorway. "Where is everybody?" He looked around, perplexed. "What are you all doing in here? Having a wake or something?"

This tasteless remark seemed to just hang in the air, obscenely, for a long moment until Babs took charge. "Caspar, you'd better come in. We're waiting for the police and I'm sure they'll want a word or two with you."

"Me? Why me?"

"Because you're here," Babs said curtly. "And Regina's office has been trashed."

"Oh, no, you don't! You're not sticking me with it. I didn't like the bi—her, but I didn't kill her and I haven't violated her office."

Georgia rose and took his arm, hissing, "Shut up, Caspar."

"Why should I? This whole gang would love to blame everything on me, and you're playing footsie with them."

Jane observed the others. Whitney Abbot was simply staring at the brother and sister, but there was a muscle twitching in his jaw. So there was some emotion in him after all. Lisa was looking away, out through the small, dusty window that overlooked the back parking lot, as if she couldn't bear the sight of Caspar. Babs was shaking her head in disgust, and Jumper was regarding Caspar with interest, as though taking mental notes. Derek Delano seemed immune from the emotions of the others and was frankly ogling Sharlene, who was wringing her hands in despair and looking unintentionally vulnerable and sexy.

"What are you doing here, Snellen?" Jumper asked.

Caspar whirled on him. "Jeez, Cable! What are you today?" He glanced contemptuously at Jumper's black leather jacket and pants.

Jumper grinned. "A lot of things. An attorney. A witness. A member of the board. And a man with a few questions. I might point out to you that all of the rest of us have a good reason for being in the building. But you don't."

"I've got the right to be here. I paid my stupid fee," Caspar said childishly.

"Your fee doesn't entitle you to be in the staff area," Babs said.

"I'm *entitled* to be anywhere I damned well please," Caspar snapped. "This is my great-grandfather's building and his money you're all spending like it's water. Money that should be, and will be, mine. Just because that Palmer woman sucked up to my batty old aunt—"

"Caspar!" Georgia all but slapped her hand over his mouth. "That's enough!"

Surprisingly, he clammed up and looked at her with something that might have been fear.

"Georgia," Babs said, "take him out into the hall and wait with him there."

Georgia bridled at being given an order, but apparently decided it was a good idea just the same. Gripping his flabby arm, she shoved her brother out of the room.

"Disgusting man," Babs muttered.

"Why is he still free to roam around?" Whitney asked Jumper in a voice harsh with self-control. "What's the matter with the police that they haven't got him behind bars? And speaking of the police, when are they going to allow us to have the funeral? This is intolerable."

"They say they can't release the body until all their tests have been completed," Jumper replied. "Maybe by Thursday."

Lisa suddenly put her face in her hands and gave a strangled sob. This so disconcerted all of them that they froze for a moment. Then Babs went over to her and led her out of the room.

Sharlene swayed a bit and sat down at the board table. Derek sat down beside her and put his arm around her. She tried to pull away from his touch and as she did so, Jumper rose and said menacingly, "Take your hands off her, Delano."

"Jesus!" Derek said, making an elaborate show of moving

away from Sharlene. "What's the matter with everyone? Can't a person even comfort somebody in distress?"

"Save your comfort for Georgia," Jumper said. "Sharlene, come with me and I'll get you a warm Coke out of that foul machine."

They departed, leaving only Jane, Shelley, Whitney, and Derek. "So much for keeping all the suspects together," Derek said with a laugh. He rose and shot his cuffs. "Well, I've got work to do. I'll be in my office if the police ever show up."

Whitney, apparently in an effort to ignore them all, had booted up the computer and was looking over the information Jane had spent the morning entering. He was nodding approval. When Derek had gone, he closed the file and sat back in his chair wearily.

"Do you need any help planning the funeral?" Shelley asked.

For the first time, he smiled. "Thank you. No, I don't think so. Lisa's taking charge. She's an organizer and has known Regina much longer than I have. Knew her favorite music and flowers and so forth."

"What about Regina's family?" Jane asked.

"She hasn't much family left. Her parents are gone and she was an only child. Just a few cousins and an aunt and uncle in D.C.," he said. "Her uncle is a senator. Her late father was a congressman."

"I had no idea she was from such a prominent family," Jane said.

He merely nodded, as if it were a given that any woman he'd considering marrying would have to be. Or perhaps,

Jane thought, she was misjudging him just because he looked so overly well bred.

"Doesn't always hold true, does it?" she mused. "Good background, I mean," she added, glancing at the doorway through which Caspar and Georgia Snellen had passed moments earlier.

"Bad apples," Whitney said curtly. "Happens in the best families."

"When were you and Regina to have been married?" Shelley asked.

He looked offended at the bluntness of the question and answered stiffly, "We hadn't set a date yet."

"Oh, I must have misunderstood," Shelley said. "I thought you were to have announced your engagement at the ground-breaking."

"You didn't misunderstand. That was our intention. We just hadn't decided on a date."

"I guess Regina wasn't in any hurry to get married," Shelley remarked. "What with having a good job and her own home and—"

"If you'll excuse me?" he said, flipping off the computer and rising. "I believe I'll wait by the front door."

"That's a pissed-off architect," Jane said when he was out of earshot. "What did you do that for?"

"I just wanted to get some idea of what he was like, and he's wrapped in so many layers of social respectability, I figured making him mad was the only way."

"Well, the making-him-mad part sure worked. What did we learn?"

"That he's a snob."

"Right. So?"

"I don't know. What if he found out that Regina wasn't what she was supposed to be? Maybe she was from the wrong side of the tracks."

"Was she?"

"I'm being theoretical, Jane."

"Well, theoretically, then, I imagine he'd break the engagement rather than kill her. And it probably wouldn't have been hard to break it off. Sharlene said Regina was hesitant anyway."

"Yes. And that really got under his skin, didn't it?"

"Well, it would, Shelley. If he really loved her, which we have to assume he did—in his own upper-crusty way—it must have been painful that she wasn't snatching the ring from his hand and shopping for a wedding gown."

"But why wasn't she, Jane? He's a catch. Rich, good-looking, respectable. I've seen his picture in the society section of the paper any number of times. Always heading up one charity ball or another."

"Maybe she wasn't madly in love with him."

"Then why would she bother with him at all?" Shelley asked. "She was an attractive, intelligent woman; had a good job, social position of her own—if that mattered to her. I admit I didn't know her at all well, but she didn't strike me as the type who was panting after marriage. She was well into her thirties. If she'd wanted to marry, she must have had plenty of chances before."

"Biological clock?" Jane suggested.

"Maybe. Or maybe she really did love him, but knew something about him that made her wary."

"Like a crazy wife locked up in the attic?"

"Jane, you're being silly!"

"And you're really stretching your imagination to the breaking point because you don't like Whitney Abbot."

Shelley grinned. "No, I guess I don't. I wonder why that is."

"Because he wouldn't let you bully him."

"*Moi?* A bully? Jane! Oh-ho," she finished, glancing past Jane to the door.

"Who have you been bullying now?" Mel asked from the doorway. "And where is everybody?"

Chapter**11**

Having determined the rest of the day was ruined for working, Jane and Shelley left the Snellen, resolved to make up for lost time tomorrow.

Jane snagged her younger son as he was leaving for the swimming pool and made him go shopping with her for new school clothes instead. For the first time in history, he didn't object. She came out of the mall an hour later, blowing on her credit card as if it were singed.

"Thanks for the cool clothes, Mom," Todd said.

"They're not cool clothes. They're ridiculous and you'll probably get sent home from school to grow into them, but you're welcome anyway."

"Drop me at the pool?"

She nodded and turned the car in that direction. "So long as you're home in time for dinner."

"What's for dinner?"

"Tuna casserole."

"Yuck!" he said. "I mean, oh, yum!"

"You know perfectly well you love my tuna casserole. You're just programmed to say yuck."

She dropped him off and went home, dragging his new clothes inside and dumping them at the foot of the stairs. Her daughter, Katie, ever alert to the sound of shopping bags, galloped down the stairs. "You went shopping without me!" she said accusingly.

"For Todd. You're this weekend."

"Mom, I can shop for myself. Why don't you just give me the money and save yourself the trouble of coming along?"

"Nuh-uh. Unless you can do it on fifty dollars."

"Fifty dollars! I couldn't even get decent shoes for that."

"That's exactly what I'm afraid of."

"Come on, Mom. You only want to buy me geeky-looking stuff."

"I thought only boys could be geeks," Jane said, perplexed. "And you're the one who wants all that clunky, no-color, ugly unisex stuff, not me."

Katie rolled her eyes. "Yeah, you'd have me in perky little white sandals and pink dresses with matching ribbons in my hair if you could. Mom, you're okay, but your sense of style is twenty years out of date."

"But my checkbook's not," Jane said firmly.

This was such an old argument that either one of them could have recited her part and the other's in her sleep. Often Katie actually seemed to enjoy the familiar dispute. Today she wasn't in the mood. She followed Jane into the kitchen. "What's for dinner?"

Jane sighed. "Tuna casserole. And you like it, too, no matter what you say."

"I think I'll eat at Jenny's house."

"Jenny's mother might have an opinion on that."

"I'll call." But before she could pick up the phone, it rang. Todd, reporting that his friend Elliott had invited him home for dinner. After ascertaining that Elliott's mother theoretically knew about this, Jane put away the tuna and pasta. Next time they asked what was for dinner, she'd lie. Her older son, Mike, was working as a delivery boy for a fancy deli and usually got dinner as part of his pay, so there was no point in cooking for him. In fact, she'd order out from the deli as well, she decided, after giving the contents of the refrigerator a once-over.

She'd just settled down an hour later with a Reuben sandwich and the deli's special homemade potato chips when Shelley knocked at the kitchen door. Jane waved her in.

Shelley had brought her own enormous coffee cup and set it down across the kitchen table from Jane. "Well, you'll be glad to know I did a Good Thing," she said. "After you left the museum, I went back in and apologized profusely to Whitney Abbot for upsetting him. I was gracious. He was even more gracious. All is sweetness and light between us."

"But you still suspect him?"

"Of course I do. But I can't think of a good reason, except that he's a prig."

"And I still think you're on the wrong track. From all I've heard about Regina, she and Whitney Abbot were perfectly suited. Remote, formal, socially acceptable, ambitious—"

"But, Jane, that's precisely the point! If they were such an ideal couple, why the shilly-shallying on Regina's part about getting engaged and setting a date?"

"Maybe she had a secret dream of a dashing reprobate

sweeping her off her prim feet. Not such a bad dream, or an uncommon one."

"Are you telling me you're turning Mel in for a pool hustler?"

Jane laughed. "Not quite. Have a potato chip."

Shelley pointed at the shopping bags heaped at the bottom of the stairway. "What's all that?"

"Clothes for Todd. Nasty clothes. Cost a fortune and none of them fit. The trousers all fall down in folds around his feet, the shorts bag halfway down his calves, and the pullover shirts all look like I bought them at a Big and Tall store. Waste of fabric and he looks like a bag lady in them. Not only that, they're all brown or gray or black. I tried to slip a slate-blue item past him, but failed."

"He'll be right in style and look exactly like the rest of his friends."

"I always thought one of the primary things about human nature is that we'd all like to look better than our friends— if it's not too much trouble."

"Not for teenagers. Frankly, I like the baggy stuff. At least for the girls. I don't want Denise inflaming the hormones of some gropey boy."

Jane nodded. "I remember quite a lengthy discussion a couple years ago with Katie about a pointy-boobed corset she actually thought I was going to let her wear over her clothes. I guess this baggy stuff they all wear is an improvement. But Katie wants me to spend a fortune on combat boots. Real combat boots! Jeez!"

There was another knock at the door and this time Jane went to open it. Mel stood on the step, a grin on his face and a paper bag from Burger King in his hand. "Can I eat here?"

WAR AND PEAS

"Sure. If I'd known you were coming, I'd have ordered you some real food."

Shelley and Jane were bursting with questions, but knew better than to interfere with his meal. He polished off the burger and fries and looked longingly at the remaining quarter of Jane's sandwich, which she turned over to him.

When he was done and had put his plate in the sink, he sat down and said, "You two look like vultures. Very attractive vultures. What do you want to know—that I'm free to tell you?"

"Everything," Jane said.

"The gun was from the museum—a .41-caliber percussion pocket pistol, made by Henry Deringer in Philadelphia, probably in the 1850s."

"How far away was it fired from?" Shelley asked.

"Can't tell. It wasn't too close because there weren't powder burns on her clothing, except some on her sleeve, nowhere near the wound. That was, we assume, from a reenactor who shot a blank past her, but close up."

"I thought forensic people had formulas and things to figure out how far away the gun was," Jane said.

"Not in this case. They don't see derringers involved in homicide cases much anymore. The last one that comes to mind is Abe Lincoln. You see, this old gun didn't fire cartridges. The way it works is that you pour loose gunpowder down the barrel and then ram a round lead bullet wrapped in a piece of cloth down on top of the powder. Then you put a small copper percussion cap containing a mercury fulminate on a nipple under the hammer. When the hammer falls, it detonates the mercury fulminate and a flame flashes through a hole in the nipple into the rear of the barrel. That sets the gunpowder off and sends the bullet on its way."

"So if you don't know how much gunpowder the murderer used, you can't tell how hard the gun shot, so the modern formulas don't work?" Shelley asked.

Jane looked at her with amazement.

Mel nodded. "Exactly. And they don't know much about spherical lead bullets anymore, either."

"I thought things were supposed to be simpler in the olden days," Jane said.

"They probably were," Mel said. "A modern firearm is a lot more complicated. You just don't have to know as much about it to fire it. Think of them as more 'user-friendly.' "

"But only a 'gun nut' would know how to fire the old one," Jane said.

Mel shook his head. "You'd be surprised how many people know about guns. Anyone who works in a museum, probably. And a lot of other people, too."

"What about the second reenactment?" Shelley asked. "The one that was filmed."

"No help at all. And before you ask, we've run down nearly everyone who was watching the first time and nobody had a video camera. One woman had a still camera and took a few pictures, but they're all of the soldiers, not the civilian reenactors."

"Go back to the gun," Jane said. "Could it have been fired from the woods instead of on the field?"

Mel nodded. "Afraid so. And nobody admits to having been in the woods except the reenactors, if that's the next question."

"It was. What about the museum case the gun was in?"

"No fingerprints whatsoever. A few fibers of paper towel stuck in the edges. Somebody went to considerable lengths to clean it up. And that might not have been deliberate. The volunteers say they often go around with a glass cleaner and paper towels when they're not guiding tours. With so many cases and so much glass, it's a constant job. One of the tour guides thinks she might have cleaned that case last Friday, but can't remember if the gun was in there or not. She had no reason to pay attention."

"Doesn't firing a gun leave powder on your hands?" Shelley asked.

Mel nodded. "It does. But by the time we had an idea of what had happened, almost all the museum people who participated had gone to that mobile home, taken showers, washed their hair, and so forth. We didn't even test anyone. If we'd tried to bring in a case on the basis of traces of gunpowder, we'd have been laughed out of court. Everyone who participated probably had some powder on their clothes and hands."

"So much for science," Shelley said. "What about alibis?"

"Just as bad," Mel said. "Babs, Sharlene, Lisa, and Tom Cable were right there on the field. No alibi at all, but all four of them didn't do it. Georgia says she was buying cotton candy, which seems so out of character that I almost have to believe her. Derek says he was in the museum's mobile home by himself. He didn't like admitting it. I think he was up to something he shouldn't have been, like pawing through the women's clothes left in the mobile home. Or maybe he's lying."

"What about Caspar Snellen?" Jane asked.

"Vague. Looking around the fair," Mel replied. "Could be true."

"And Whitney Abbot?" Shelley asked sharply.

Mel smiled. "Your personal favorite, I take it?"

Shelley shrugged.

"Says he arrived a few minutes before the reenactment, but had misunderstood the time it was to happen and sat in his car doing some paperwork. Had the engine running, windows up, and air-conditioning on full blast. Says he didn't even hear the battle. Claims the first he knew there was something wrong was when the ambulance and police cars arrived. And that, too, could be true."

"I must say I'm surprised at how well you're taking all this," Jane commented.

"I'm only second in command," Mel said. "It's nice for a change."

"The guy with the food poisoning's back on the job?" Jane asked.

"Home. Sticking close to his bathroom. Trying to run a murder investigation by phone. I wouldn't trade places with him for anything."

"What about the incident today, with Regina's office?" Shelley asked.

"Don't know much of anything yet. Babs and Sharlene are trying to put everything back together and figure out if anything's missing. I've got to go back there in a little while. But Sharlene said there wasn't anything obviously gone. Regina's most important papers were accounted for before I left."

"What could someone have been searching for?" Jane

mused. "Or was it a search rather than plain old vandalism?"

"Looked to me like a search. There were lots of things that could easily have been broken or torn up, but weren't."

"It must be connected to her murder," Shelley said.

Mel shook his head. "Not necessarily. Maybe someone saw the fact that the office was unoccupied as an opportunity to grab something they didn't want anyone else to know about."

"Like what?" Shelley asked.

"Oh, suppose someone had written a letter of complaint about one of the employees or volunteers. Regina might have called the accused person on the carpet and said, 'Straighten up or I show this to the board.' "

Shelley nodded. "I guess that's possible. So who could have been in there, unnoticed?"

"Nearly anyone," Mel said. "The last time anyone admits to being in that office was Sharlene, first thing in the morning. She says nothing was disturbed then and she's fairly certain she locked it back up, but not positive. And even if she did, the keys were hanging on that board all day. Makes you wonder why they bother with keys."

"Still, it must have taken nerves of steel to go in there during the day with people roaming around," Jane said. "If somebody had walked in on the search, how could it have been explained?"

"At least one person involved with the museum has already proved to have pretty good nerves," Mel reminded her. "Committing murder in front of an audience."

Chapter**12**

Jane and Shelley arrived at the museum early the next morning, determined to accomplish a lot of work. Sharlene was the only one there. Today she wore a hot-pink floral dress that turned her hair to glorious flame. "Wow!" Jane said. "You're gorgeous. I'd give anything to have your coloring!"

Sharlene blushed. "I don't feel gorgeous. I'm exhausted."

"You were here late last night?"

"Until eleven. I got Regina's office straightened up. The policewoman with me helped a lot."

"What was missing?" Shelley asked.

"Nothing that I could tell. The police dusted for finger-prints, which made more of a mess to clean up."

"Did they say whose prints they found?" Jane asked.

"Oh, everyone's. Regina's office was always open to the staff. She didn't consider it all that private and everybody was in and out all the time."

"That board meeting yesterday—what happened?" Shelley asked.

WAR AND PEAS

"They appointed Derek acting director. Babs made it clear that it wasn't a permanent appointment," Sharlene answered. "He wasn't at all happy about that. I guess Babs is going to work on finding someone from outside to interview. I wouldn't be surprised if Derek isn't already sending out résumés. I hope he is. I don't know what I'd do if he stayed."

"You couldn't work with him?" Jane asked.

"Oh, I could, I guess. Rather than starve. But I wouldn't like it. He's so—so creepy. I always feel like he can see my underwear. Or is wishing he could. And he's so egotistical. Most men when they make a pass and get rejected are either embarrassed or angry. But Derek can't *be* rejected. He just doesn't see it. He keeps trying again and again. And I'm in no position to be as rude to him as I'd like."

"You could file a sexual harassment suit," Shelley suggested.

"I'm not so sure I could," Sharlene said, and surprised them by adding, "I've looked up the laws and there are too many shades of gray. He's not stupid, you know. Everything could have an innocent interpretation. Like yesterday, when I got upset and he put his arm around me. I knew it was just a grope. He could say he was being sympathetic and supportive. And he does things like suggesting that business conversations be conducted over lunch. I'd call it a date. He could come back and say it was lunchtime anyway and he was only trying to avoid wasting valuable time. Oh, well. Like I say, I don't think he'll be around for long. I can stick it out."

They'd been heading for the boardroom as they talked. After they had entered and Sharlene turned on the overhead lights, Shelley said, "I think I left that clipboard with the forms in the basement. I'll be right back with it."

"No, turn on the computer and fix me a cup of coffee," Jane said. "I'll get your stuff."

When she returned a minute later, she didn't have the clipboard. Sharlene was gone and Shelley was waiting patiently. "Jane, what's wrong?"

Jane spoke quietly. "Come back to the basement with me."

She led the way down the stairs and stood aside for Shelley to enter. "Uh-oh," Shelley said, surveying what she could see of the room. "Another search?"

Cartons were open; boxes were overturned; old files were strewn around the floor.

"Apparently somebody thought whatever they were looking for in Regina's office might be down here instead," Jane said.

Shelley sighed. "Mel isn't going to like this."

He didn't.

"Could any of you tell if something was missing?" he asked when he was shown into the basement half an hour later.

Sharlene shook her head. "I haven't been down here much lately. I can't understand it. There's nothing of value here. These are rejects and old records and things people have donated that we don't dare get rid of but have no use for."

Shelley had been picking her way delicately through some of the mess. "I don't think anyone was after an object. The boxes and cartons are all labeled, and the only ones that have been opened are marked 'Books' or 'Files.' And not recent files, either."

"How odd," Jane said. "If somebody's looking for something old, why would they start in Regina's office? And if they're looking for something recent, why bother to come down here? It doesn't make sense."

"Two different people looking for two different things?" Sharlene suggested.

"Maybe, but it seems unlikely," Jane said. "The only common thread seems to be Regina's death. Whoever is doing this presumably couldn't do it before she died. Or maybe they had no need to."

Mel wasn't interested in this speculation. He turned to Sharlene. "Would there be any way to know what's missing, if anything is?"

"I don't think so," Sharlene said. "Unless Jane and Shelley filled out inventory forms on some of the things down here."

"No, we didn't," Jane said.

"You two were down here yesterday?" Mel asked.

"Yes. We came upstairs when Sharlene discovered the mess in Regina's office and we didn't come back until this morning," Shelley said.

"So anyone in the building yesterday afternoon could have come down here," Mel said.

Jane thought back to the gathering in the boardroom while they had waited for him. Georgia had taken Caspar out of the room. Babs had left with Lisa. Jumper had removed Sharlene. Derek had gone to his office and Shelley had driven Whitney away. "Yes, anyone could have zipped off for a minute," she admitted.

"This took more than a minute," Mel said.

"Not necessarily. Not for the person who knew what they were looking for," Shelley said.

"Or if there were two of them," Jane said, thinking about the pairs of people who'd left the room. "And maybe it wasn't in the afternoon. Could someone have hidden down here and done this overnight?" she asked Sharlene.

"Maybe. We have a janitor who comes in three nights a week, but last night wasn't one of them."

"But, Mel, if someone had stayed here overnight, wouldn't they still be in the building?" Jane asked.

Sharlene cleared her throat and looked upset. "They could have left. What with police coming and going during the evening, I locked the door, but turned off the alarm system so it wouldn't be set off by accident. Nobody could come in, but anyone could have gotten out. I'm awfully sorry."

Mel sighed. "I'll call in a report."

Jane rescued Shelley's clipboard and went back to the boardroom. Shelley returned to taking inventory of a second-floor room. Jane greeted Heidi, the stuffed cat, and as she settled in at the computer, Derek Delano came into the room with a file folder. "Oh, I didn't know anyone was here," he said. "Are you going to be long?"

"All day," Jane answered. "Do you need me to leave?"

"No, no! I just have a few papers to copy. No need to disturb you at all," he said.

He sounded so guilty and nervous that Jane smiled to herself and guessed that he was using the museum's copier to run up duplicates of his résumé. Sharlene had underestimated his intelligence—or his cheapness. A bright person would have sprung for the money at a copy shop.

"Can I help you?" she asked with sweet maliciousness.

"No! I'm fine. Just go on with your work," he said, sounding downright panicked.

Jane went on with her data entry as the copier hummed and papers rustled. He must be blanketing the world with job applications, she thought. He finally finished and stacked his copies in a box. Just as he was slipping the lid on, the door opened and Jumper Cable appeared. Today he had on a Stetson hat, lizard-skin cowboy boots, Western-cut tan trousers, and a plaid shirt with pearl buttons.

"Secret stuff going on?" he said cheerfully. "Why was the door closed?"

"Was it?" Derek said, checking the copier to make sure he hadn't left a page in it.

"Is Detective VanDyne around?" Jumper asked. "I told him I'd meet him here."

"I think he's talking to Sharlene," Derek said. Out of the corner of her eye Jane noticed that he'd put his box of résumés on a chair and put a box of blank copy paper on top of it. "Is this about the basement?" he asked Jumper, joining him at the board table.

"Yup," Jumper said.

"It's up to the board and the police, of course, but I wouldn't waste much of anybody's time on trying to figure it out," Derek said. "Seems to me that somebody's just plain nosy. But I think, considering everything, we ought to get some locks changed and make better use of the security system."

"I agree with you," Jumper said, sounding as if he were surprised to find himself in accord with Derek.

"Listen, Cable—about this acting-director position—any

idea how long before the board makes a permanent selection?"

Jane kept on working at the computer. Apparently a woman at a keyboard was much like a woman driving kids in a car. She ceased to exist as a hearing human entity.

"I don't know," Jumper answered, seemingly as unaware of Jane's presence as Derek was. "As you must know, we keep a file of applicants for positions here and will probably be asking them to update their material if they're interested. I've suggested putting an ad in trade publications, but Babs disagrees."

"You do know I'm interested in the job, don't you?" Derek's tone was unattractively wheedling.

"Of course," Jumper said pleasantly. "It's always best to promote from within, if possible."

"I've—well, I glanced through that applicant file this morning. As acting director, I think I'm entitled to." He waited a moment to see if Jumper would dispute this, but Jumper said nothing. "I don't think you'll find anyone in there with my credentials," he continued.

"Possibly not," Jumper said. Jane wondered if Derek could also hear the wary tone creeping into Jumper's voice. "Your academic background is impeccable. Downright impressive, in fact."

"Thanks," Derek said.

There was a long silence and then Jumper spoke again, slowly, choosing his words with great care. "There are other considerations as well."

"Like what?"

"Oh, public-relations aspects of the job—"

Derek sounded relieved. "Right. You saw that television

spot I did two weeks ago about the Pea Festival, didn't you? If I do say so myself, I think I did a good presentation on that."

"It was excellent," Jumper said. "But the anchorwoman who interviewed you is a friend of mine. She called me later and said you'd tried to hit on her off camera."

"Hit on her? That's nuts! Why do women think that any good-looking man who's pleasant to them is trying to score? Jeez! Well, let me tell you, your anchorwoman friend is a frigid bitch. It's like Regina, getting all uptight. Of course, she was a lesbo."

"What?"

"Well, it figures, doesn't it? A woman that age who's never been married?"

"I doubt that her fiancé would agree with that," Jumper said coldly. "Derek, this attitude of yours—that everything is sexual and that any woman who doesn't fall for you is frigid or a lesbian or imagining what your motives are—counts against you. Badly. All your academic credits fade away when the board has to consider possible suits against you and the museum."

"What are you saying—*cowboy?*" he said sarcastically. "That I'm not going to be appointed director?"

"It's not up to me. But you shouldn't count on my vote. And as attorney for the museum, I'll warn the others of the liability."

"*I'm* a liability? Look here, you've got a board with a lawyer who likes to dress funny, an old broad who bumped off her husband—oh, you didn't think I knew about that, did you?—and Georgia out there doing fund-raising and keeping half the money for herself. And you call *me* a liability?"

Jane nearly slid off her chair, but forced herself to pretend she wasn't listening. She fancied that Heidi the cat looked more interested than she did.

Derek got up and grabbed his box of résumés so violently that the lid flew off and papers fluttered everywhere. He snatched them up roughly, jammed them back in the box, and stomped out of the room.

Chapter 13

"**He said what?**" Shelley said, whispering but managing to sound hysterical at the same time.

Jane had found Shelley hunched over a glass case, trying to transcribe the information on the labels of various kitchen tools onto her data forms. There was a school group going through the room. "Come out in the hall," Jane whispered back. When they were alone, Jane said, "Jumper and Derek were having an argument. It started out with Derek trying to find out if he had any chance at being appointed director. Jumper wasn't committing to anything, but said something about Derek's 'way' with women, and Derek made some crack about how some television friend of Jumper's was frigid and Regina must have been a lesbian if they failed to respond to his overtures, and that really pissed Jumper off and he came right out and said he'd oppose Derek's appointment and tell the board he'd get them all sued if he got the job—or something like that. And then Derek said how could Jumper call him a liability when the board had an old lady who killed her husband. And a crack about Georgia raising funds and keeping part of the money."

"Whew!" Shelley said, glancing around furtively to make sure nobody could overhear them. "How did Jumper react?"

"I don't know. I didn't dare look at him. I think they'd both forgotten that I was even in the room. I could see only Derek in my peripheral vision. He got up and dropped his résumés—"

"Résumés?"

"That's what he was doing in there, I think. Copying résumés."

"Georgia playing tricks with the money doesn't surprise me a bit," Shelley said. "But what on earth did he mean about Babs? He was talking about her, wasn't he? There isn't another older woman on the board, I don't think. Didn't Jumper react to that at all? Ask Derek what he meant or anything?"

"I imagine he looked surprised. Derek said, 'You didn't think I knew about that, did you?' But it was all over too fast for Jumper to say anything. Derek blew all this steam and flounced off."

"Didn't Jumper notice you then?"

"I don't know. I just kept typing random nonsense and a minute later, I heard Jumper walk out of the room. I deleted the computer mess I'd made, then came looking for you."

"Did anyone else hear this?" Shelley asked.

"I have no idea. The door was open and Derek was talking loudly. I suppose if anyone was in the hallway, they could have heard."

"I think we had better take Sharlene out to lunch and find out what this is all about."

"But carefully. Derek might have just made it all up to shock Jumper. We don't want to help him spread a rumor."

Shelley set up lunch with Sharlene while Jane went back to work, and they all met at the front door of the museum a little after noon.

"This is so nice of you two," Sharlene said.

"Not at all. You deserve a treat," Shelley said. "This has been a tough week."

Shelley had made reservations at a very nice Italian restaurant a few blocks away that was run by a friend of her husband's, so they were ushered to the best table as if they were royalty. Sharlene wanted to know what everything on the menu meant, and the young waiter, who was goggle-eyed at her lush, if somewhat unusual, beauty, was more than happy to oblige her. They finally settled on their orders and Sharlene asked them how they were coming along on the database project.

Surprisingly, for all the revelations of the morning, Jane had managed to get a lot of information entered and reported her progress. "But do you have any idea how many thousands of individual 'things' the museum has?" Jane asked. "If it's just Shelley and me, it'll take us months and months to even start making a dent."

Sharlene nodded. "Next week we'll have lots more help. When school starts, more volunteers will come on. At least they've said they will."

They fell into a discussion of volunteer work in general and the difficulties institutions were having now that so many women, even those with young children, were joining the work force. Shelley fidgeted, anxious to get to the object of this luncheon. Sharlene finally gave her an opening.

". . . and in the summer, a lot of teachers help us out. And often take on a year-round role when they retire."

"Babs McDonald was a teacher, wasn't she?" Shelley asked.

"Yes, a college history professor," Sharlene said. "She even wrote a couple of textbooks. But I don't think she ever considered teaching as a full-time job. She didn't have to. She comes from a lot of money, I hear, and the research and writing were her main interests. At least that's the impression I've always had."

"She's a remarkable woman," Jane said.

"Is she married?" Shelley asked.

"No. Widowed. A long, long time ago. It's a tragic story."

"Oh?" Jane said encouragingly.

The waiter brought their salads and Jane was afraid the food might steer the conversation away from Babs, but after tasting and raving about the salad, Sharlene returned to the subject without any prodding. "She was married during World War Two. A whirlwind courtship, I imagine, with her young man going off to war. Anyway, they were married only three days or so when he left. And he was gone for a whole year. When he came home on leave for a couple days, some friends of theirs threw a big party for them. Sort of a delayed wedding shower, I think. And on the way home their car went off the road and her husband was killed. Babs was pretty badly hurt, too."

"How horrible!" Jane said, thinking this didn't at all match Derek's version. "Was that her only marriage?" Maybe it was another husband he'd referred to.

"Oh, yes. She must have loved him so much she could

never love another man," Sharlene said, her enormous blue eyes misting romantically.

They ate in respectful silence for a few minutes before Shelley asked, "How do you know about this? Did Babs tell you herself?"

"Oh, no! I'd never ask her about anything so personal and painful. She never mentions her husband. No, I found an article about it when I was cataloging some of our old newspapers a couple years ago. I made a copy of it, just because it had to do with someone associated with the museum, but I never said anything to her about it."

Their lunch arrived with a flourish. Lasagna for Shelley, eggplant parmigiana for Jane, and fettuccine Alfredo for Sharlene. They concentrated on eating for a while, until Shelley said with elaborate casualness, "I wonder if anyone else at the museum knows."

"Knows what?" Sharlene asked, nibbling on a piece of garlic bread.

"About Babs's marriage."

Sharlene considered. "Miss Daisy knew—she was friends with Babs since they were girls—and so I imagine Ms. Palmer knew. She was close to both of them. And probably Tom, just because he knows everything."

"What about the others?" Jane asked. "Like Derek Delano?"

"Oh, I don't think so. How would he? Babs was never very friendly toward him. She surely wouldn't have talked about it to him. And I don't think anybody else would."

"And Georgia?"

"Oh. I see. Yes, Georgia would know, I guess. She was Miss Daisy's niece and would have heard."

So that was how Derek had learned the information, Jane thought. But why did his version have Babs "murdering" her husband when it was simply a car wreck?

"Why are you asking about all this?" Sharlene was suddenly wary.

"No reason," Shelley replied. "It's just such a moving story . . ." She paused, took in Sharlene's skeptical look, and glanced at Jane, who nodded. "That's not true," Shelley said. "Jane overheard an argument between Jumper—Tom, rather—and Derek this morning. Derek made a nasty crack about Babs and said she murdered her husband."

Sharlene was horrified. "No! What a terrible, terrible thing to say!"

"He was very angry," Jane explained. "Jumper had told him that he wouldn't support his appointment as permanent director, and Derek was just flinging insults left and right."

Sharlene's pretty face was flushed. "That makes me *so* mad!"

"I'm sorry we upset you," Jane said. "But you obviously didn't believe why we were asking questions. Still, look at it this way—Derek has probably ruined any chance he might have had of staying on at the Snellen. It was an ugly thing to say, but it almost certainly means he's not going to be your boss for much longer."

The redness in Sharlene's face faded somewhat and she smiled. "Thank you, Jane. For telling me the truth and for making me feel better. I'm sure Tom won't let him be director. Tom thinks the world of Babs. I guess nasty things sometimes happen for good reasons, don't they?"

"Sometimes," Jane agreed. Then she said to Shelley, "Are you going to let the rest of the cats out of the bag?"

"Georgia, you mean?"

"What about Georgia?" Sharlene asked.

"Derek said something about Georgia, too," Jane told her. "About how she cheated on the fund-raising money and kept some of it herself. Do you suppose that's true?"

Sharlene looked down at her lunch for a long minute, then sighed. "I shouldn't talk about this, but I think everybody already knows. Including the police. Yes, Georgia often seems to turn in less money than is actually raised. I take minutes, you know, for the board meetings, and I've heard the rest of them question her about her figures. And I've taken enough accounting courses myself to see that she's probably skimming."

"The whole board knows this?"

"Knows? I'd say suspects strongly. Georgia's not stupid, you understand. Caspar is, but Georgia isn't."

"And they let her stay on the board?" Shelley was shocked to the core.

Sharlene nodded. "For a couple reasons. For one thing, she doesn't seem to keep much. Not enough for the risk she's taking. It seems to be a game or something. Just to feel that she's putting something over on them, maybe. I don't know."

"It would probably cost them more to prosecute her than she's taken, then?" Shelley asked.

"I imagine so. And until Miss Daisy died, nobody wanted to embarrass her by throwing Georgia off the board. Miss Daisy knew Caspar and Georgia were both crooks and all, but that would have made it public."

"Still—" Shelley said.

"The thing is, Georgia is good at fund-raising," Sharlene

explained. "Very, very good. She knows lots of people with lots of money to give away. Before Miss Daisy's bequest, the museum might have gone broke without Georgia. Miss Daisy wouldn't have let it really happen, of course, but she'd have been awfully disappointed in all of us. So the board is grateful to Georgia, see?"

"But they have plenty of money now," Jane said.

"Yes. That's true." Sharlene thought for a long minute, then said, hesitantly, "I guess you might as well know— there was supposed to be a regular board meeting the week after the Pea Festival closed. I typed up the agenda. One of the items Ms. Palmer had on it was 'Replacement of board member.' I didn't ask, of course, but I assumed that meant Georgia. Of course, Ms. Palmer died, and now all the normal business is sort of on hold and they're only having emergency meetings to cope with it."

"This agenda you typed up," Shelley said. "Had everyone on the board seen it?"

"Oh, yes. The bylaws require that I send it to everyone a week before the meeting."

"So Georgia must have also suspected that Regina wanted her out?" Jane said.

"Yes, I imagine—" Sharlene stopped and her eyes got very wide. "You don't think Georgia shot Ms. Palmer—?"

"Sharlene, somebody did," Shelley said.

Chapter 14

"**Nobody would kill** to keep a position on a volunteer board," Jane said.

They'd returned to the museum, and Jane and Shelley were alone in the boardroom again. Sharlene had thanked them effusively for the lunch and gone back to work in Regina's office.

"In fact, I would think there would be a fair percentage of the population that would do anything up to and including murder to get *off*," Jane continued.

"But not if it was because of embezzlement," Shelley argued. "Off the board and into jail isn't a very good option."

"But if the rest of the board had accepted Georgia's doctored version of her fund-raising all these years, wouldn't they have just held the threat over her head to force her to resign? Making a big deal of it would make the museum look incompetent."

"Probably, but could she count on that? Maybe not," Shelley said. "Suppose Regina had evidence that she'd stepped up her cheating and had really taken them to the cleaners on something? Or what if Regina had already privately warned her that she should resign and Georgia had indicated she wasn't going to and Regina had vowed to Reveal All?"

"Still—killing her wouldn't solve Georgia's problem, just delay the revelation. Surely if Regina knew about some grand-scale cheating, the accountant on the board knew about it too."

"The accountant's in Alaska, remember. Regina might have been the only one who knew, and told Georgia she was going to give her findings to the accountant when he returned."

"Why wouldn't Regina call and tell him right away, before having a showdown with Georgia?"

Shelley shrugged. "Maybe she couldn't reach him. Or maybe she knew he wouldn't have had his books with him on vacation. Why would he? I don't think this museum is his primary business. It's probably just a volunteer, pro bono kind of thing he does on the side."

"Hmm. That might explain Regina's office being searched, wouldn't it?"

"Yes, it could have been Georgia trying to find whatever evidence Regina had."

"But then what about the basement? Why would Regina think, with the whole museum in which to hide something— presuming Regina had the *need* to hide it—that anybody would choose the basement? Surely there's a safe somewhere. Or if Regina had been concerned about a single copy of something being stolen, wouldn't she have made a copy or two and spread them around?"

WAR AND PEAS

"I don't know," Shelley said. "Maybe Georgia just lost her head and tried to think of where she herself would have hidden something."

Jane shook her head. "I don't know that I'd believe that. I think Georgia—or whoever it was—had good reason to believe something she wanted was down there."

"Perhaps," Shelley said.

"I can't quite picture Georgia as a murderer for some reason. She's obnoxious and, it seems, a petty thief—"

"Maybe not so petty," Shelley said. "If Regina had been driven to get rid of her after all these years of graciously overlooking her pilfering, there might have been a lot of money involved. And keep in mind that Regina was killed during the Pea Festival. A big money-raising opportunity for the museum. Couldn't it be that Regina had already seen evidence of Georgia's thievery?"

"Like what?"

"I don't know!" Shelley said, becoming a bit defensive. "Maybe people pay to rent those booths and Regina found out from one of them that they'd paid Georgia a whole lot more than they're supposed to?"

Jane nodded. "I guess that could be. You know what I'm really having trouble with? The idea of the board allowing her to get away with stealing. I can't imagine Jumper or Babs letting it go, and I've never known an accountant who could ignore something wrong with the books. Getting the information out of Sharlene wasn't all that easy, so I don't think she's lying, but couldn't she be mistaken?"

Shelley stuck her purse in the drawer next to where Jane was working and started assembling her papers. "Could be. It might be a matter of interpretation. It's possible they suspected her, but couldn't find any evidence at all. You know, I was thinking about Sharlene's interpretational abilities when she was telling about Babs's husband."

"What do you mean?"

"Well, she said she got her facts from a newspaper article. But newspapers, even then, didn't gush about whirlwind romances and great loves of people's lives. Not even folksy local papers, I'd guess. I think she was putting a lot of her own romantic spin on the story."

"Wonder if she kept the article," Jane said. "She said she made a copy. But whatever it says, I'd bet you're right and she read a lot into it."

"I'll ask her if she still has the copy next time I run into her," Shelley said. "We better get on with what we're supposed to be doing or we'll be here until they cart us off to the nursing home." She tapped down her pile of forms, adjusted them carefully on her clipboard, and turned toward the door.

And stopped.

"Sharlene? What's wrong?" she asked.

Sharlene was standing in the doorway. She was dead white and holding a crumpled piece of paper out in front of her by one corner. "I—found this," she whispered.

Jane rose. "Put it down on the table, Sharlene."

They crowded around and gazed. It was a piece of plain white typing paper. On it were the typed words: "Regina, you can't do this to me. If you try, I'll stop you."

"Where did you find this?" Shelley asked.

"In the dumpster behind the building. I was putting out trash from my office and sort of daydreaming, and I looked down and saw this."

"What else was around it? Whose trash?" Jane asked.

Sharlene looked confused. "I don't know. I didn't think. I just picked it up—"

"Sharlene, you need to call the police again," Shelley told her. "Jane, do you want to stand guard over this and I'll go stand by the dumpster until they get here?"

Jane picked the paper up carefully, holding it exactly where Sharlene had already touched it. She put it behind the stuffed cat and began entering information on the computer. She had a strong feeling that when Mel arrived, it would be best if she were busily engaged in something—anything—that had nothing to do with the murder. She was typing like her life depended on it when Sharlene escorted Mel into the room a little while later. "Where's that paper, Jane?" Sharlene asked.

"Behind the cat," Jane said without looking up.

The officer with Mel lifted it carefully with tweezers and they left the room without a word.

An hour and a half later, Jane was leaning back and feeling supremely smug over having nearly caught up with all of Shelley's forms. Lisa Quigley came into the boardroom. "You haven't seen Derek, have you?" she asked.

"He hasn't been here," Jane replied.

"Sharlene says she's accumulating a bunch of calls he needs to return. Maybe he went home early." Lisa poured herself a cup of coffee. Jane stretched and got up to refill her cup as well.

"Caspar's roaming around here again," Lisa said, pinching the bridge of her nose as if to compress a headache. "He said the police are back."

"Yes. Sharlene found a note."

"A note?"

"Yes, a note that looked like a threat to Regina. It was in the dumpster out in back."

"*Note!*" Lisa exclaimed. "About Regina not doing something?"

"Yes, it was," Jane said. "What's wrong? How did you know?"

"Oh, my God!" Lisa had turned alarmingly pale. "I knew about that! And I didn't say anything! I'd forgotten! Oh, how could I—?"

She rose suddenly and started pacing. "I told her she should take it seriously, and then *I* went and forgot about it? Is there still a police officer here?"

"Yes, there is," Mel said from the doorway. "When did Ms. Palmer get this note?"

Lisa was wringing her hands. "A week ago? No, longer than that. Let me think for a minute. It was a week ago Monday, I guess. I'm so sorry. I should have told you right away."

"What did Ms. Palmer think about the note?" Mel asked.

"She laughed it off. Almost. She handed it to me and said that somebody was playing childish games. She was sort of irritated, I think, but not really upset."

"And you were?"

"Well, of course. I don't remember exactly what it said, but it looked to me like a vague threat."

"Are we talking about the same note?" Mel asked her, unfolding a photocopy of the note and putting it on the table.

Lisa studied the copy. "Yes, I think so. It was just a line or two like this."

"Did she say who she thought wrote it?" Mel asked.

Lisa shook her head.

"Did you have an opinion?"

She looked at him. "Do I have to answer that? I had a guess, but it was just a guess."

Mel let her reply go. "Are you aware that this was typed on the machine in Ms. Palmer's office?"

"No, of course not. Are you sure?"

"Quite sure. Who had access to that machine?"

Lisa shrugged. "Practically anyone, I suppose. Regina only locked her office at night, and I don't think she always did that. Except for the typewriter and answering machine and such, there wasn't anything valuable. Valuable to anyone else, I mean. And she kept her door open during the day unless she was having a private conversation."

"Even when she was out of the office?"

"I—I think so. I never especially noticed. Sharlene would know better than I do."

"So Ms. Palmer handed you the note?" Mel said, shifting gears abruptly.

"Yes." She looked at him questioningly and then the light dawned. "Oh, fingerprints. Yes, mine are probably all over it."

"And you handed it back?"

Lisa thought for a minute, obviously having trouble concentrating. "I guess I must have. Or maybe I just put it down on her desk. I have no idea. Oh, I feel so bad and stupid about this. Would it have helped if I'd told you about it sooner? I can't imagine how I could have forgotten it, except that so much else has happened—"

Mel refolded the photocopy and put it back in his inside jacket pocket. "No, I don't think it would have changed anything. Did you notice anything different about her after she got this note? Like locking up her office or taking any special care for her safety?"

"No, not really. But then, it was the week that the Pea Festival started. Everybody's frantically busy then. If she did anything differently, I'm not sure I would even have noticed." Her eyes filled with tears again and she said, "I should have paid more attention. She was my best friend. I should have looked out for her better."

Jane handed her a napkin from the stack beside the coffeemaker. "Lisa, we can't always look after ourselves as well as we might, let alone other people. You can't hold yourself responsible."

"I know—but still—"

"Jane, I have a few more questions to ask Ms. Quigley," Mel said.

"And you want me to get lost. Okay. I need a break anyway," Jane said.

●

───────────

Chapter15

Proud of her day's work and prevented from going back to the computer because Mel was using the boardroom, Jane went home early. It was an unusually cool, dark afternoon with rain clouds threatening. Remembering that trash day was tomorrow, Jane decided she might as well break down and clean out her station wagon, which was in its usual state of looking like a motorized wastebasket. She went indoors to try to recruit "kid help," but found three notes on the kitchen bulletin board.

Gone shopping with Jenny and her mom
—Katie

At Elliott's
—Todd

Joined the French Foreign Legion
—Mike

She rounded up her car-cleaning supplies, invited the cats to come help, went back out to the driveway, and started removing everything that looked useful or important. She stacked things on the cement by ownership: some of Katie's notebooks that had been in there since the last day of school nearly three months earlier; Todd's emergency backup supply of Legos in a clear plastic box; some cassette tapes of Mike's that had been kicking around gathering dust since he got his own vehicle. She decided the movie section of the paper that was a month old was trash, as were a truly disgusting number of fast-food bags and cups.

Jane discovered a number of perplexing things in the car. A long-overdue library book titled *Lilies: The Gardener's Best Friend*. What on earth had inspired her to check that out and why, having gotten it, hadn't she taken it inside and read it? Her garden could certainly use a best friend. The book went into the pile of things to go back into the car when she was through cleaning.

To her embarrassment, she also found the telephone bill that had caused such a hassle. The phone company had threatened to cut her off for nonpayment and, in high dudgeon, she'd indignantly insisted that she'd never received it. They'd sent another, which included a late-payment charge that Jane had fought with a high-minded arrogance that even Shelley had admired. Jane quickly tore up the bill and stuffed the bits into the trash bag, fearing that even as she was doing so, some official of the telephone company was watching through binoculars and saying into a walkie-talkie, "Yup, she had it all along, just like we thought."

There were treasures, too. Shelley had convinced her a couple of weeks earlier that she needed a bird feeder and there it was, still in its box, waiting to be filled with the special seed mix Shelley had recommended. Unfortunately, there was a hole in the bag of seeds that looked suspiciously chewed. Did she have a critter living in the car? She opened all the doors, giving any resident wildlife the opportunity to escape, and walked around the outside of the house looking for the best place for the bird feeder. She decided on a spot in front of the window the kitchen table sat next to and felt terribly smug that she was able to find a screwdriver and get the bracket in place without any trouble.

She was just filling the feeder when Shelley pulled into her driveway, which adjoined Jane's. "It looks like your car exploded—all the doors standing open that way," Shelley said. "And there are the wildcats picking over the remains."

Max was sniffing at the glove box and Meow was sitting on the top of a headrest, a golden ball of fur surveying a new kingdom. "Wonder what they'd think of Heidi."

"Who's that?" Shelley asked.

"Mr. Snellen's stuffed cat," Jane said. "I wonder if they'd let me borrow it for a night, just to see if Max and Meow recognize that it was once a cat."

"You've grown attached to that dead cat, haven't you?" Shelley said. "There's no accounting for taste—or lack of it."

"But it has such a nice story. It's sort of like that picture Sharlene has of Mr. Snellen himself. Except that Heidi's three-dimensional."

"And hairy," Shelley said. "And probably infested with God knows what."

"Then Max and Meow would be sure to like it. They adore infestations."

"Jane, what did you think about that note Sharlene

found?" Shelley said, putting down her purse and helping Jane get the spilled birdseed into the feeder.

Jane went to retrieve a plastic bucket from the garage to put the birdseed bag into and said, over her shoulder, "I've been trying not to think of it, to tell the truth."

"Does that have a lid?" Shelley asked. "If not, you're going to have a garage full of happy, overweight rodents. Why are you not thinking about the note?"

"Because it confuses me," Jane said, rummaging around for the lid, which she was sure existed somewhere. "Ah! Here it is. I'm not so sure that note was really a threat— just a sort of warning. But there's a big difference."

"Well, there can be . . ." Shelley said hesitantly.

"Shelley, suppose it was about something fairly innocent. What if, for example, Regina told somebody she was going on a diet and the other person left her that note?"

"Jane, I only saw it for a minute. Exactly what did it say?"

"I'm not sure I remember exactly. Something like, 'Don't do it or I'll try to stop you.' See what I mean? It could just be Babs or somebody making a little joke meaning she'd start leaving candy bars on Regina's desk. It wasn't signed, so presumably Regina knew who had sent it and what it meant. But Lisa didn't take it that way—"

Jane repeated the conversation she and Mel had had with Lisa.

"So Lisa had seen it and was really upset by it?" Shelley said.

"She was upset today and claimed she took it seriously when Regina showed it to her. But that might only be in light of what happened later. After all, Lisa forgot about it until I mentioned that Sharlene had found it. Then she got really bent out of shape, blaming herself for not making Regina take it more seriously."

"But Regina didn't acknowledge knowing who it was from or what it was about?"

"Lisa says not. And Mel asked if she, Lisa, had any thoughts about who typed it, and she said she did, but didn't want to say."

"This is strange," Shelley said, snapping the lid onto the birdseed bucket and hauling it to Jane's garage. "Where are you hanging the bird feeder?"

"By the kitchen-table window."

Shelley picked up the feeder and went around the house. "Omigawd! Did you put up that bracket yourself?"

Jane preened. "I'm not barefoot and pregnant anymore, Shelley. I'm a modern, liberated woman who can put a couple screws into a wall all by myself."

Shelley grinned. "What's next? Repairing washing machines? Overhauling carburetors?"

"No, so far I'm only up to spark plugs. But anything's possible. What was going on at the museum when you left? Had anybody admitted to writing the note?"

"Not that I know of, but I got my information from the woman in the gift shop. That's what makes me wonder if the note wasn't a real threat. If it were simply a joke, why wouldn't whoever wrote it just say so?"

"Maybe they have and the gift-shop woman hasn't heard about it yet. And think, Shelley, if you wrote somebody a note like that to be funny and the person turned up murdered a few days later, would you leap right in and say you wrote it?"

"Both of us would. But we wouldn't have killed anyone, so we'd have no reason to worry."

They walked back around to the driveway. "But what if we'd done something else bad?"

"What do you mean?"

"Suppose Regina told Georgia, for instance, that she was going to expose some financial hanky-panky and Georgia wrote that note, but then somebody else killed Regina for some other reason entirely. If I were Georgia, I wouldn't want to admit to the note and then have to explain to everybody what it was all about. I'm just not convinced that the note necessarily had anything to do with Regina's death. And there's a lot of further confusion in my mind about Regina's office being searched. Was that note what somebody was looking for? If so, they obviously didn't find it. But why go looking for it in the basement?"

"I know, I know," Shelley said. "I can't make any sense of it, either. I'm starting to get paranoid and think everybody's up to something shady."

"I wonder if it comes down to Regina herself," Jane said, putting the library book back in the car and closing the doors after making sure the cats were out. "I can't face vacuuming this now. I'll try to bribe one of the kids to do it. Let's go in and sit down. I think it's about to rain."

When they were settled at Jane's kitchen table, and had duly admired the birdless bird feeder, Shelley said, "What do you mean about Regina?"

"Just that we didn't really know her at all. We're relying almost entirely on other people's impressions of her, and they're not all the same. And yet I don't feel like I've got a balanced picture of what she was really like, merely a bunch of conflicting ideas. How long will it be before birds come?"

"Any second now."

"Really?"

"No, Jane! Maybe tomorrow. Maybe next week. You're right about Regina. Sharlene thought she was a goddess—remote, perfect, sort of bloodless, but kind. I'm not sure that's what Sharlene thinks, but that's the impression I had."

"Right. Me, too," Jane said. "But Derek seems to have seen her as a stumbling block to his sexual and professional ambitions. He tried to seduce her out of her job and it didn't work. He thinks she was cold and probably imagines she was as ambitious and aggressive as he is. And for all we know, he was right."

"And we're told that Caspar Snellen hated her, too, claiming that she'd tricked Miss Daisy into giving the money to the museum just to further her own ambitions. Regina's ambitions, I mean."

Jane nodded. "Caspar's a creep, but even creeps can be right occasionally."

"Probably not in this case, though," Shelley said. "Everybody seems to agree that Babs McDonald was a lifelong friend to Miss Daisy, and if Babs even suspected that Regina was conning her friend, she wouldn't have been supportive of her. And she must have been, or Regina wouldn't have kept her job all this time."

"I suppose so," Jane allowed. "But Babs said herself that she didn't approve of Caspar or Georgia. She wouldn't have wanted them to have Miss Daisy's money to throw away. Maybe she just turned a blind eye—"

"I don't think Babs ever turned a blind eye on anything," Shelley said.

"You say that only because you want to be her when you grow up," Jane said.

Shelley laughed. "I guess I wouldn't mind. I sure hope I have her figure, her hair, and her wardrobe when I'm her age."

"You can't fool me. You can buy all that stuff. What you want is her 'presence.' "

Shelley looked disgruntled at this blunt truth. "I wonder what the real story is about her husband's death. I didn't have any opportunity to ask Sharlene about the newspaper clipping."

"Let's stick to Regina," Jane said. "Whitney Abbot thought well of her. He wanted to marry her. More than wanted to, he planned to. I can't imagine him getting swept away by anyone who was less than perfect."

"Yes, but like we said before, if he felt he'd been made a fool of in some way, or tricked by her, it might be a motive for murder."

"A pretty thin one," Jane said. "My take on him is that he'd consider social shunning a fate far worse than death."

"Lisa, of course, thought well of Regina," Shelley said. "But what about Jumper?"

Jane shrugged. "No idea. He was Miss Daisy's attorney and probably would have dissuaded her from giving her money to the museum if he thought there was anything dishonest or disreputable about Regina."

"What if he was in love with her?" Shelley said suddenly, looking as if she'd taken herself by surprise with the thought.

Jane stared at her friend for a minute as if she'd gone completely mad. "I—you take my breath away. What an extraordinary idea! But if he were, why would he kill her?"

"Because she was going to marry Whitney. They were going to announce it at the groundbreaking party. The if-I-can't-have-you-nobody-can thing. Jane, that makes more sense than anything else. It's passion. Even the most normal people can be driven to murder by passion."

"I don't like it," Jane said. "I really, *really* don't like this idea, because I do like Jumper."

"But that's got nothing to do with it," Shelley said. "Give me a good reason why it couldn't be Jumper."

"I can do that," Jane said after a moment's thought. "Because I think he's in love, all right. With Sharlene. She's certainly in love with him. And what's more, I think it's up to us to do something about it!"

"Jane, will you please make up your mind whether you're a sleuth or a matchmaker?"

"I can be both. I told you, I'm a modern woman."

Chapter16

The rain was only a drizzle and stopped just as Todd arrived home. Jane managed, by a balanced combination of bribes and threats, to convince him to take the hand vacuum outside and finish the car cleaning. She got busy fixing her own special macaroni and cheese casserole (part of the bribe), and because this was a great favorite with the kids, all three of them managed to fit dinner at home into their social schedules.

Jane was loading the dishwasher when the phone rang.

"Jane, this is Babs McDonald. I hope I'm not interrupting your dinner."

"No, we just finished."

"Good. I wonder if I might ask you a favor. I'd like to meet you to discuss something. I understand from Jumper that you were present this morning when he had a rather unpleasant discussion with Derek Delano—"

"I was," Jane said hesitantly. So much for thinking she'd made herself invisible.

"And I presume you've discussed it with your friend Shelley."

"I—er, yes."

"Quite natural that you would," Babs assured her. "Then perhaps you two would be willing to get together with me so I can tell you about killing my husband?"

That's what she said," Jane said, glancing around Shelley's pristine kitchen resentfully. Shelley's house was always clean, yet Jane almost never actually caught her cleaning it.

"So what's the plan?" Shelley asked.

"You know that family-style restaurant across the street from the mall? We ate there once and the entree was awful, but Babs swears the desserts are wonderful. We're supposed to meet her there at eight-thirty. You will come, won't you?"

"I wouldn't miss it for the world."

They arrived a few minutes early and Babs was already in a booth at the far wall. She gestured regally, and like schoolgirls summoned to the principal's office, Jane and Shelley joined her. They made awkward chitchat while giving their orders—at least it was awkward on their part. Babs didn't seem the least disconcerted.

"I know it's a ghastly place," she said quietly so the waiter wouldn't hear, "but the grandson of a friend of mine does the desserts and they're superb. I recommend either the lemon meringue pie or the raspberry torte, and the brownie fudge cake is the best chocolate I've ever tasted."

They each ordered one of these three suggestions and kept the conversation relentlessly impersonal until the desserts arrived and had been duly tasted and shared. Finally, Babs said, "I don't normally have any particular urge to talk about myself or rehash my own history, but in light of what Jumper told me, I thought I should explain—"

"You really shouldn't feel you have to tell us anything if it's too painful to talk about," Jane said.

Babs smiled. "I've found there are very few things too painful to discuss. To do, perhaps, but not to discuss. And I wouldn't be speaking of it at all except that I feel you are both honorable, trustworthy women. I'm seldom wrong about these things. And, Jane, in case you're wondering if I'm about to confess something that will put you in an awkward position with your friend Detective VanDyne, let me assure you that I'd be entirely content to tell him as well, should he wish to hear it firsthand."

"Thank you," Jane said weakly.

Babs set her fork on her plate, placed her elbows on the table, and crossed her hands elegantly. "I grew up in privileged circumstances and was a 'good girl.' My parents were fine, if rather snobbish, shallow people, and I was their only daughter. I adored them and did all I could to please them. Bobby McDonald was the only son of their closest friends, and it was assumed we would marry eventually. I was content with the idea. He was bright, charming, good-looking. I convinced myself I was in love with him, although I had no idea what love meant. It was merely girlish romanticism.

"When the war started, I was only nineteen. Too young to marry under normal circumstances, but the war wasn't normal. And while nobody ever admitted it openly, Bobby's parents pushed for the marriage to take place before he left. I think their pride in their name and heritage was so great that they feared it would die with him, should he not survive. Perhaps they were in the grip of parental premonition and hoped that I would conceive a grandson.

"A big society wedding was planned, with a leisurely honeymoon in California, but Bobby's orders were changed and we had only two days to stage the thing. I wanted the big wedding, the bridesmaids, the big white dress and everything. It was the dream of every girl of my class in those days, but I was pressured to go along with the slapdash alternative. I was such a 'good girl,' and there was an element of romance at that time in hasty marriages."

She stopped speaking as the waiter approached and poured everyone fresh coffee. When he'd gone, she continued. "I discovered on my wedding night that there was a truly savage side to this handsome, charming boy I had married. I don't mean fumbling, insensitive overeagerness. I mean true viciousness. I won't bore you with the details, but if there is such a thing as a pornographic horror novel, I lived it. For two days, that seemed like an eternity in hell. And then he left to go be a hero. I moved back in with my parents. I worked as a volunteer at a hospital. And I prayed every night that the next day would bring the telegram saying he was dead.

"But the telegram didn't come. A year went by. A year in which I relived those two days over and over and over and grew more terrified—"

"Why didn't you tell your parents?" Shelley asked quietly. "Surely they'd have wanted to save you. The marriage might have been annulled—"

Babs shook her head. "Nice girls didn't talk to anyone about sex in those days, especially not their parents. And they wouldn't have believed me even if I could have gotten the words out. Of course, the words weren't in my vocabulary then. Besides, he'd had the cunning not to leave marks any place that I'd dream of showing anyone. None of us had ever seen him be anything but polite and cheerful—before. No. They'd have thought I'd gone mad. And it would have destroyed a lifelong friendship between them and Bobby's parents. Most of all, I was still a good girl.

"Anyway, Bobby was wounded very slightly and, while recovering in a field hospital, got a severe ear infection. His father pulled all sorts of strings and got him transferred home to the States for treatment. His train arrived at five o'clock in the afternoon. Our whole social set turned out to meet the returning hero, and there was a dinner and reception planned for him at the country club. I spent the evening in the bathroom, being sick. He spent his time drinking. His parents wanted us to stay at their house, but my parents, with the best intentions in the world, had rented a hotel suite for us so we could be alone together, which was the most horrifying thought in the world to me. I was dizzy with fear.

"I'd driven my car to the club, and since I was sober, I drove us to the hotel. It was December. Cold and icy. I can still remember the faint burned-sugar smell my car heater made. Sometimes I catch a whiff of an odor like that and it still makes me sick."

Jane was feeling sick herself, just listening and imagining the terror that the innocent young Babs must have felt. But Babs was speaking calmly now, far more calmly than Jane could have.

"We left the country club and I was trying to concentrate on my driving," Babs went on. "The road was treacherous.

WAR AND PEAS

And as we reached a spot where there had been many winter accidents due to a sharp curve and a steep embankment, Bobby reached over and yanked my skirt up and plunged his hand into my crotch. I had a second of frigid terror, and then a stunning realization. This was going to be the rest of my life. And I couldn't live such a life. I can't tell you how liberating it was. I was suddenly calm, rational, and happier than I'd ever been. I knew how to get out of the nightmare and it was easy. I'd *die*. It was so simple! And I'd take him with me so he couldn't ruin anyone else's life when I was gone. It was the only truly spiritual moment of my life. I thought God had set it up for me—the cold, the icy road, the sharp corner, the embankment. It was all so perfect that it had to be a Divine Order. So I wrenched the wheel sharply to the left. And killed Bobby McDonald."

She paused and took a sip of coffee. "But not myself," she added. "Obviously. When I recovered, I still felt I had done God's work. I believe it to this day. And the months I was in the hospital gave me time to realize other things, too. That I could never go back to being anybody's good girl. That my body and my mind were in my own sole care and would remain so. I would never let another man have control of either. I would create my own life the way I wanted it to be."

Jane discovered she'd been holding her breath for quite a long time.

Shelley started to speak, but for once had no words.

Babs put out both her hands and Jane and Shelley each took one. Babs squeezed them firmly, then let go. "My dears, this is harder on you than me. I'm sorry I upset you, but I thought you should know. And maybe, too, I just needed to tell it one more time. Selfish of me, but I'm of an age to feel entitled to a little selfishness. To finish the story, I couldn't go back to my parents' house and wasn't well enough to live alone for several months, so my dear friend Daisy took me in and cared for me. Not only physically, but mentally as well. Although she had no interest in an academic life, she was the one with the perception to realize it would suit me. She gave me college catalogs, and helped me find my own apartment when I was well enough. It hurt my parents, I know, that I turned to a friend instead of them, but that was how it had to be."

She smiled radiantly at her companions and signaled the waiter. "I believe we each need a new cup of coffee, if you wouldn't mind," she told him.

"I wonder if you're aware that Sharlene read an old newspaper article about your accident and has a very different interpretation of it," Shelley said in voice that trembled slightly.

"Dear Sharlene. I'm sure her story is very pretty and romantic," Babs said with a fond smile. "She's a pretty person all the way through. I've seldom known anyone with so much intelligence and such pure goodness. It's a rare combination. As for Derek—"

The waiter came back with clean cups and a steaming carafe. When he'd cleared away the used cups, Shelley asked, "How would Derek have known anything about this?"

"I suppose Whitney Abbot might have mentioned it and Derek did a little digging. Derek might have been taking a shot in the dark, or he might have heard the alternative version."

"Alternative version?" Jane repeated.

"Yes. You see, there was a bit of scandal that followed the 'accident.' Apparently someone started a rumor—or it might have had an element of truth, I didn't care which—that Bobby had fallen in love with one of the Army nurses who treated him in England. According to the gossip mill, he'd told me that he was going to divorce me and marry her. This was supposedly the reason I'd been sick all evening, you see? And because I couldn't live without him, I'd tried to kill us both. There were no skid marks on the road and that added fuel to the rumor. Daisy told me about it and we had a good, if rather cynical, laugh out of it."

"How would Whitney have known?" Jane asked.

"Oh, he's part of the same crowd. His grandmother gave one of my wedding showers. And fifty-year-old gossip is as good as a recent scandal among the old families. Now, I'm starting to feel my age. I'd better get on home. I'll see you both tomorrow. Stay and finish your desserts."

And with that, she put a twenty-dollar bill on the table, gave them a quick glance defying them to object, and left.

Jane and Shelley stared at each other for a minute. Finally Jane said, "Shelley, I don't think you *can* be her when you grow up."

Shelley shook her head. "No, I don't think so, either."

Chapter 17

Jane and Shelley entered the boardroom Wednesday morning just as Lisa was coming in for a cup of coffee. Lisa was looking distinctly haggard, a bit wrinkled, and angry. Sharlene was already in the room, filling a cup herself.

"Sharlene, I just got a call from that Harriman woman about her mother's wheelchair that she's determined to donate to the museum," Lisa said. "I thought Derek was going to take care of it."

"He was supposed to. I put her on the list of calls to return yesterday," Sharlene replied, rummaging in a cabinet for more sugar packets. Today she was wearing a shimmery dark purple blouse and a black skirt. Whether by intuition or by study, she made the very best of her stunning coloring.

"Did he return any of the calls?" Lisa asked irritably.

"I don't know," Sharlene said. "I didn't see him all afternoon. I put the list on his desk. I'll go see if it's still there." She was back in a moment. "No, sorry. The list's right where I left it and nothing's checked off."

WAR AND PEAS

"And he's not here yet this morning?" Lisa asked.

"Apparently not," Sharlene said, emerging triumphantly from the cabinet with a rather elderly box containing individual sugar packets. "At least his car's not here. I checked. Of course, he lives close by and usually walks to work unless he has a lunch appointment. Do you want me to call him?"

"No, don't bother. But I hope you'll make sure Babs and Jumper know that their acting director isn't doing his job." She glanced at Sharlene. "I'm sorry. I'm not cranky with you. It's just that everything's so difficult. You'd think the least Derek would do is show up for work. I was hoping to get away for a while myself this afternoon and rest a little, but if I have to take up the slack for him—"

"Lisa, go back home now, why don't you?" Sharlene suggested. "You look so tired, and if you wear yourself to a nub and get sick, it'll be harder on everyone. I'll return his calls and explain that due to what's happened, we're a little behind this week."

Lisa smiled weakly. "Not now, but maybe later I'll take you up on that." She patted Sharlene on the shoulder, picked up her coffee cup, and left.

Sharlene approached the table, and as Jane backed up to get out of her path, she bumped into the counter where the computer was. The stuffed cat tumbled off and she barely managed to catch it before it hit the floor. "Poor old Heidi," Jane said, standing it upright and back in place. "Your stuffing must be clumping up to make you rattle that way." She gave it a pat on the head and adjusted it so that the base was a little more firmly set and wouldn't take another header.

"I really wish Lisa would go home," Sharlene remarked, stirring two packets of the slightly lumpy sugar into her coffee. "She looks exhausted and miserable. And it's not like her to be snappish, even about Derek."

Jane thought back to Lisa's suggestion that Derek might be responsible for Regina's death and then trying to deny it. "Has she never gotten along with him?" she asked.

"Oh, not to say didn't get along. But they've never been friendly."

"Did he make passes at her, too?" Shelley asked.

"Maybe. I don't know. She never mentioned it. I think she just found him distasteful. And being friends with Ms. Palmer, I'm sure she knew what trouble he'd been to her."

"Trouble. I hear the word and think of Derek," Babs McDonald said from the doorway. "Jumper isn't here yet, is he?"

"No," Sharlene said. "Is he supposed to be?"

"I'm meeting with him this morning, but I'm terribly early. Jane. Shelley." She smiled greetings at them. "Did you get the rest of the paperwork I asked you for, Sharlene?"

"Yes, but I don't want you to trouble yourself with it right now," Sharlene said. "Everybody has much more important things to worry about than what classes I'm going to take in the fall. I'm awfully grateful for your taking an interest, now that Ms. Palmer's gone, but—"

"No buts, my dear. Just bring me the folder. Were you discussing Derek when I came in?" She turned to Shelley to ask this question. Sharlene hastened away.

"I wasn't discussing anything," Shelley said with a grin. "For once. But Sharlene and Lisa were talking about him.

He apparently failed to return a bunch of phone calls yesterday and hasn't shown up yet today."

"Doesn't surprise me a bit," Babs said. "If he has any sense at all, he's home phoning for job interviews. Still—it's irritating that he can't even return calls. I guess I'll do them instead. For all I know, he's quit and simply hasn't bothered to tell us."

"You don't seem especially distressed about that," Shelley observed.

"I'm not," Babs said frankly.

"Won't it be hard on everyone until you can find another director?" Jane asked.

"I don't think so. I believe we have a line on an excellent candidate already. And I've reached the other board members and they're FedExing proxies to Jumper. If Derek's quit on his own, it will be easier to replace him. Meanwhile, I'll go do his job."

"What's this, Jane?" Shelley asked when Babs had left. She was holding up an old, flat book.

Jane looked at it for a minute. "I don't know. Oh, yes, I do. I picked that up in the basement the other day when we were thinking about starting to inventory. I didn't have a clipboard. I thought it would make a good substitute. What is it?"

Shelley set the book on the table and opened it. She flipped a few pages. It was a handwritten ledger of some kind, done in an old-fashioned, somewhat florid style of writing. Some pages were filled out. Others had only a line or two on them.

"Hard to read," Jane said. "I wonder what it is. Oh, I see why it's hard to read." She laughed. "It's in German. At

least parts of it are." She looked more closely. "Shelley, I'll
bet . . ."

Shelley nodded. "Yes. Auguste Snellen's genetic experiments. Look, some of the pages have the same kind of numbers that are on the little labels on the pea cabinet. And
some have a name, too. Here—Snellen's Early Spring, and
here's one called Daisy's Favorite. How sweet. He named a
pea for his granddaughter."

"This is a treasure," Jane said. "And I was using it just
as a flat surface. I'll put it up safely. Remind me to give it
to Sharlene when things settle down."

They put their purses away, poured themselves coffee,
and as Shelley gathered her paperwork, Jane booted up the
computer and sat down, after sliding the ledger book in
under the board the stuffed cat was mounted on. Shelley
started to leave the room, but hesitated and came back.
"Jane," she said quietly, "you don't think—no, that's too
stupid."

"You can say stupid things if you want," Jane said, grin-
ning. "I don't have a secret tape recording going."

"Smart aleck. I was thinking . . . could that book be what
somebody was looking for in the basement?"

Jane looked at her for a minute. "I wish I did have a tape
recorder now. Why would anyone care enough to be sneaky
about it?"

"You're right. Its only value is probably sentimental and
historical. Forget I asked."

Shelley had been gone only a few minutes when Sharlene
came back into the boardroom. "Babs, I just—oops. Where'd
she go? Tom called and said he was tied up in court for
a while."

"She said she was going to make some of Derek's calls," Jane said over her shoulder. "Maybe she's in his office."

"Thanks. I'll look for her there. Isn't that sweet of her?" Sharlene said, bustling out of the room.

Jane smiled at the cat. "Heidi, would you have the nerve to call Babs McDonald 'sweet'? I wouldn't."

Babs was back in an hour. "Any sign of Jumper yet?" she asked Jane.

"Not that I know of," Jane said. She joined Babs at the board table and said, "Since you've been so frank with Shelley and me, do you mind if I ask you a question?"

"Fire away," Babs said cheerfully. "If I don't know the answer, I'll make one up."

"Well, I have the impression that the board of directors thought that Georgia Snellen was helping herself to some of the funds she collected for the museum."

It would be too much to say Babs looked surprised, but she was mildly startled. "I believe 'think' is the operative word. There was never any evidence of cheating. Merely suspicions. For example, the cash collected at any given activity always slightly exceeded the number of receipts—"

"I don't understand."

"Then think back to your work at the booth at the Pea Festival. We're a nonprofit organization—a 501 (c) (3) in IRS talk—and if somebody buys an item from the booth, the person working there is supposed to offer them a receipt for the difference between our actual cost and the amount we sell it for, and the purchaser can take it as a tax deduction."

"Oh, dear. We didn't do that," Jane said.

"You were working under emergency conditions. I don't imagine anyone thought to tell you. Anyway, most times people don't want to wait for a receipt, or it's such a small amount they don't think it's worth figuring into their taxes. And lots of times, because it's a charitable institution, people often deliberately overpay or refuse to take their change back. So you end up with more cash than receipts to account for it. And Georgia always *did* end up with excess cash. But not as much as we'd expect. The gift shop, for example, averages about twelve percent extra cash. Georgia always turned in about three percent extra. And that's not proof of anything. You could postulate that Georgia has such an abrasive manner that people are less likely to be generous with her."

"Yes, but I understood that she's quite good at raising money," Jane said.

Babs looked at Jane with an arched eyebrow. "That is true," she said. "But proof is proof and speculation's quite another thing." She made clear that this was all she was willing to say about the matter and Jane let it go.

"May I ask you something else, then?"

Babs nodded.

"Sharlene told me that Regina and Whitney were supposed to be announcing their engagement at the groundbreaking ceremony. But she also hinted that Regina hadn't exactly rushed into committing to marriage."

"Right again," Babs said.

"Do you know why that is?" Jane asked.

"What an odd question," Babs said. "Why do you ask?"

"I'm not sure," Jane answered honestly. "I'm just curious about Regina, I guess. I never met her, you know. But from what I hear about her, it's hard to imagine that she'd inspire murderous rage in anyone."

Babs laughed softly. "That's perilously close to damning with faint praise."

"I didn't mean it that way," Jane said.

"No, dear, I know you didn't. I can't really answer that. If Regina had confided in me why she was hesitant about marrying, I wouldn't feel I could break that confidence. As it happens, she didn't. She wasn't a confiding sort of woman. Frankly, I have a theory about it, but it's merely theory and it would be irresponsible to put it out as anything else—"

"Babs. There you are," Lisa said from the doorway. "Did you get the message from Jumper? He said he's on the way and please wait if you can."

"Thank you, Lisa. Sharlene told me. Lisa, I don't mean to be insulting, but you look exhausted. Why don't you go home and rest?"

"I was just planning to." She jingled her car keys in her hand to illustrate the truth of this.

As Lisa started to move away, Babs said, "I'll walk you out. I need to talk to you about one of the phone calls I made—excuse me, will you, Jane?"

Lisa and Babs went off together and Jane went back to work. But something was nagging at her. Something she couldn't quite get hold of. She sat back and closed her eyes for a minute, trying to tease the idea out of hiding, but couldn't lure it into the light. It was something that Shelley had said recently. She opened her eyes and looked at the stuffed cat. "Heidi, if only you could talk. Or even listen," she said. "Wonder if Auguste Snellen named a pea for you."

She returned to the computer and a moment later, as

she had hoped, the elusive idea came hunting for her. She stopped typing and got up.

She'd put the pea-experiment ledger under Heidi. She now removed it and carefully flipped through the pages. It was confusing and frustrating, the way the text went from formulae to German text to English text, but she finally found what she was looking for. Page 87 was labeled "Snellen's Little Beauty" and what's more, an envelope fluttered out from between the pages. She picked it up carefully.

It was postmarked 1934 and came from Arkansas.

Chapter**18**

"I think you might have been right. This ledger is what someone was looking for in the basement," Jane said. "That's where the old pea storage thing is, and logically the ledger was there, too."

"But what would it have to do with Regina's death?" Shelley asked. Jane had located her in a History of Pitchforks display at the north end of the second floor.

"Probably nothing, but it would explain a little mystery. If, in fact, we discovered that the search in the basement *didn't* have anything to do with Regina's death, it would clear out some debris—so to speak."

"I guess that's true. Okay. Let's assume for the moment that somebody was looking for this ledger—you did take it before the basement was searched, right? Assuming that, who could it be? Only you or Sharlene. You're out because you already found it," Shelley said with a smile, "and Sharlene would have no reason to be secretive about it. She'd search in a tidy manner and even if she'd been sloppy, there'd have been no reason not to admit it."

"But why just the two of us? I was sort of lurking behind a display when I heard that man telling the story about the pea. Why couldn't someone else have been lurking, or at least accidentally overhearing it, too?"

"Like who?"

"Like anybody in the building. I saw Caspar shortly before the old man told Sharlene the story. Anyone else might have been just outside the doorway. Shelley, I want to see if this ledger showing Snellen's Little Beauty actually leads us to some peas."

"And you don't want to go in the basement by yourself? All right. But let me finish with the pitchforks first. Only two more tags to go."

Jane paced impatiently while Shelley completed her work; then they headed for the stairs. As they went down the last flight, it occurred to Jane that they should have brought a key in case the storage room was locked. But fortunately, it wasn't. She turned the knob and the door swung open. Jane stepped forward into the darkness, flailing for the string that would turn on the overhead light. Just as she grasped it and pulled, her foot touched something in the middle of the floor. There hadn't been anything there the last time they were down here.

She looked straight ahead, afraid to look down.

But Shelley's surprised gasp changed her mind. Automatically stepping backward, she clutched the ledger book to her chest and gazed down in horror at a body.

Jane and Shelley gave their reports to the first police officer on the scene and were asked to wait in the boardroom. They waited. And waited. Too stunned to speak in anything but monosyllables, they sat at the table, drinking far too much coffee and listening as more sirens approached and then one departed.

After a while, Babs came in, looking ashen. She merely nodded acknowledgment of their presence and said tersely, "I'm rather glad that Daisy didn't live to know all this."

Neither Jane nor Shelley could think of any response to her comment.

Babs took a book from a shelf and sat down, pretending to read and making it clear that she wasn't in a mood to say anything more. A quarter of an hour later, Jumper joined them. He was wearing a green hospital scrub suit and his complexion very nearly matched his clothes.

"The officer outside said he could send someone for lunch," he told them dully.

They all shook their heads in the negative.

"I guess they're asking us the same things," he said. "When we last saw him. And they don't much like the idea that the last time I saw him was here, when I told him what a jerk he was. Or maybe they do like it," he mumbled, more to himself than to them. "Nothing like bagging an attorney for murder. Probably adds a full paragraph to a résumé."

"Résumé . . ." Jane murmured. "Was that what all those papers on the floor were? Derek's box of résumés?"

"Was that what was in the box he stomped out of here with yesterday?" Jumper asked.

"I assumed so," Jane said.

"Then if he was still carrying them around, that means—" Jumper stopped.

But Babs was recovering and wasn't afraid to say the rest. "It means Derek's probably been lying there in the basement since yesterday. And we've all been complaining about him not doing his job."

A sort of collective shudder ran through them.

Shelley cleared her throat and said to Jumper, "Did the police mention how—?"

Jumper nodded. "There was a blow to his head. I don't know if they've identified the weapon—"

"But his face," Jane said, shivering with revulsion at the memory. "Why—"

"The blow didn't kill him," Jumper went on. "Only knocked him out. Then someone"—he paused, searching for an acceptable word—"someone filled his nose and mouth with peas to obstruct his breathing."

"Peas!" Babs exclaimed. *"Peas?"*

"From a drawer in that big piece of furniture with all the drawers."

"I haven't been down there in years," Babs said. "What kind of furniture is for peas?"

"It's like the seed bins they used to have in hardware stores," Jumper explained. "Except instead of bins, there are drawers. Old Auguste used it to store his genetic crosses. I helped drag the thing away from the wall a couple years ago when the foundation-repair people were here to give us a bid."

Babs nodded. "Yes, I remember it now. It used to be in his office at the warehouse. Daisy took me there once and I was fascinated with it."

Jumper had flung himself into a chair, laced his fingers together, and was staring at them as if they held an answer. After a moment, he looked up at Jane. "What were you two doing down there anyway?"

WAR AND PEAS

There was only the slightest hint of suspicion in his voice, but it was enough to compel Jane to explain. They'd all find out sooner or later anyway.

"We were going to look in that pea furniture for Little Beauty. When I got here Monday, I heard a man telling Sharlene that when he was a kid during the Depression, his family had grown that particular Snellen pea one year. He said it sprawled around on the ground and was too hard to harvest, but his father had some left over that he planted as ground cover for a couple years. The man telling Sharlene about it said they grew the best potatoes in the world the next year, and carrots and beets and things, and it kept his family from starving."

Babs said, "Oh, Sharlene started to tell me that story, but the phone rang while we were talking and she never got around to finishing it."

"Carrots, potatoes, and beets?" Jumper said. "Anything else?"

Jane was surprised by the question and thought for a minute. "Turnips, maybe."

"Root crops," Jumper said under his breath.

"Anyhow," Jane went on, "Shelley and I were down there Monday and I picked up a book to use as a clipboard. And we noticed this morning that it was a ledger. I looked at it again and saw that one page of it was about the Little Beauty pea, and there was a letter in the book that's probably the one that the family's father wrote to the seed company when they lost their pea crop to the frost and wanted to order more. The company hadn't pursued growing and selling that pea because it fell on the ground. And I was just curious about it. The drawers have code numbers on them, and there was a code number for Little Beauty in the ledger. So we went to look, but found Derek instead."

"Root crops," Jumper said again. "Don't legumes leave something in the soil? Nitrogen or something? I wonder . . . couldn't this particular kind of pea have done something unusually good that caused root crops to thrive?"

"I guess so," Jane said. "I sort of knew that about beans. But I hadn't thought it out that way. I was only curious to know if there were any still left. I thought Sharlene might want to give a few to the man who told her the story. He was sentimental enough to make a trip here to talk about it and—"

Shelley interrupted her. "Jane, a plant that leaves extra nutrients in the soil could be very valuable."

"It sure could," Jumper said. "There are people patenting 'designer' plant crosses these days. I don't know enough about science or farming to actually say, but Shelley could be right. Someone who really knew his or her way around DNA might produce a patented plant that could make a fortune."

"Who else heard this man talking to Sharlene?" Babs asked.

Jane shrugged. "Anybody might have. They were in that room just off the entry. There are lots of exhibit cases in there. I stayed behind the one I was looking at simply because I didn't want to intrude."

Babs shook her head. "No, it doesn't make sense. Even I knew about legumes and nitrogen, but I can almost promise you that nobody involved with the museum is an expert on genetics and DNA."

"But an outsider might be," Shelley said.

WAR AND PEAS

"An outsider wouldn't know about the pea bin in the basement," Babs said.

"I'm not sure you'd have to be an expert," Jumper said. "It's not an area of the law I've had reason to study, but my guess is that if you had possession of the peas, you could hire an expert. Or turn the matter over to an interested scientific facility under a royalty arrangement. But you said it was during the Depression that the family grew the peas. Even if there were still seeds around, would they grow?"

"How long do peas remain viable?" Babs asked, probably knowing nobody had the answer.

Shelley spoke up. "I don't know about peas, but some grains will grow after hundreds of years."

"And even if you couldn't grow them, you might be able to clone cells to determine the genetic makeup," Jumper said. "Could that be why somebody tore up the basement the other day—looking for that ledger?"

"I'd wondered that, too," Jane said.

"And if he or she went back to search again—" Jumper went on.

"Derek might have found the searcher—" Shelley said.

"Or *been* the searcher," Jumper amended. "What if he'd overheard the conversation about the special pea and gone down to look a couple days ago? Then, when I told him that he wasn't going to be appointed director, he went back to make a more thorough search so he could steal the peas before he left?"

Jane shook her head. "No, I don't think so. There would be no reason for someone to kill him just because he was looking for the pea ledger. Unless he was in it with someone else."

"Like Georgia," Shelley said.

"We have turned into ghouls," Babs said. "This is all wild, irresponsible speculation. And it's not our job. It's up to the police."

"True," Jumper said, chastened by her tone. "But it's up to us to tell them all we know. And part of what we know is the relationships of the people here at the Snellen."

"Yes, of course. I'm sorry. Old-lady nerves," Babs said. "All right. Let's don't wander off into a science none of us knows anything about. Just look at the overall picture. If Derek's death actually did have something to do with the peas, and if we assume that his death and Regina's are connected in some way—"

"I think that's a logical assumption," Jumper said. "I can't believe we have two murderers operating independently."

"—then what has Regina got to do with the pea—what was it called? Little Beauty? That's impossible. Nobody had ever heard about it until after Regina was dead."

Chapter**19**

Jane excused herself, theoretically to visit the restroom, actually to get away from the others in the hope that her own mind would clear. It seemed that no matter how they looked at the situation, eventually they splatted up against a brick wall of common logic. She sensed that they were wallowing in a swamp of speculations where there was an answer hovering over their heads that they hadn't bothered to look at.

Or maybe she was going a tad batty herself. She wished she had a better idea of what the police knew, but she suspected that, for all their technical expertise, they were as baffled as she.

The officer lounging at the door of the boardroom let her go without any difficulty. Apparently the confinement in the boardroom was merely a suggestion, not a requirement. Jane decided to make a preventive visit to the bathroom, and when she was washing her hands, Sharlene came in, pushing the door with her derriere and holding her hands in front of her as if they were contaminated. "Laser copier dust," she explained.

Jane turned on the faucet for her and leaned back against an old steam-heat radiator under the window. "So you're being allowed to do your work?"

"Somebody has to if we're going to run the museum and get moved. Thank heaven we didn't have any tours scheduled today, since the police have closed us up."

"You're taking this surprisingly well," Jane remarked.

"No use pretending," Sharlene said, sounding a little like Babs. "I really think it's terrible that somebody killed Derek, but I can't act like I liked him just because it happened. What I think is most awful about it is that it happened *here.* This is bad for the museum. Bad publicity. Lisa's going to have a big repair job when this is all over. I'm starting to think somebody's doing it simply to ruin us. But that's silly, I know. Nobody would take horrible risks like that just to hurt the museum's reputation."

"I'm confused, too," Jane admitted. "There are too many trivial motives, real or imaginary."

"That's exactly it," Sharlene agreed. "I can't imagine killing anyone for any reason, and because we're all stuck in the middle of this, we're all thinking of really stupid reasons. It's easier with Derek than it was with Ms. Palmer."

"How do you mean?"

Sharlene was drying her hands, looking with irritation at the black dust that had stayed under her short, unpolished fingernails. "Just that for all his brains and degrees and everything, he was a couple sandwiches short of a picnic where people were concerned. Lots of book learning, but no tact, no thought for others. Nothing like Mr. Abbot or Tom, for example. They're both educated and smart, but they don't run over people. And when they make mistakes, they admit it, instead of trying to blame others."

"Mistakes like what?"

"I was thinking about Mr. Abbot and the bathrooms. I guess no one mentioned that to you."

"I don't think so," Jane said, imagining Whitney Abbot walking into a ladies' room.

"He had all the plans for the new museum done—the architectural drawings, I mean. And I had a set I was supposed to set up as a display in the main lobby. So I sort of studied them and realized there were no bathrooms on the first floor. I mentioned it to Ms. Palmer, and the next day Mr. Abbot asked me to take down the display and thanked me. He was really nice about it and explained that he'd done it on a computer and had taken out the bathrooms to change some hallway patterns and had forgotten to put them back in. He laughed about all those drains and pipes and things under the hallway."

Blaming it on the computer instead of on someone else, Jane thought to herself, but didn't say anything. A computer couldn't argue or get its feelings hurt or knock you on the head with a blunt object. At least not yet. Though she suspected that Bill Gates had some if not all of those options in the works.

"He made it sound like I'd really done him a big favor," Sharlene was saying. "He even mentioned it again yesterday."

"Yesterday?"

"He came by to get copies of some forms he needed and to remeasure the height of a couple of the taller exhibits. It's his job to make sure they can fit through doorways and halls."

"When was this?"

"Oh, in the afternoon sometime. Two? Three?"

Jane wondered if anybody had mentioned to Sharlene that Derek might have been killed the day before.

"But when Derek did something wrong," Sharlene continued, "or made someone mad, he didn't seem to notice, and if someone else said something, he started looking for someone to blame. Still, that's no reason to kill him. Lots of people are annoying and that's just life. I guess I should feel sorrier than I do. He must have had family that cared about him."

"And Georgia," Jane said.

Sharlene nodded. "In her own way. I guess she was lonely and liked having a young man take an interest in her."

"That's a kind, generous interpretation," Jane said.

"No, not really. I feel sorry for her and I think it's just as bad to feel sorry for people as it is to dislike them. But it's sad, really, when somebody tries so hard to pretend they're young when they're not. I mean, look at Georgia, then look at Babs."

"That's very perceptive. It's impossible to imagine Babs acting like Georgia at the same age."

For some reason, this gave Sharlene the giggles. "I'm sorry. It's just—well, I suddenly thought of Babs being forty or fifty and wearing poodle skirts and saddle oxfords. Oh, dear. I better not get silly or the police will think I'm nuts."

With that, she forced herself to assume a serious, businesslike expression and left.

Jane trailed along slowly, thinking about Whitney Abbot.

How could an architect forget about bathrooms? Still, she considered herself an intelligent person and she'd done a few head-slappingly stupid things in her life. Anybody could make a moronic mistake now and then. And at least he'd been nice to Sharlene about it, even if he had tried to partially blame the computer program.

Jane knew if she went back to the boardroom she wouldn't be able to do any work amid a roomful of people, so she decided to take advantage of the fact that the museum was closed and roam around on her own. She was feeling overloaded by people and opinions and facts. Especially since so many of the facts and opinions were so hard to sort out and place in one camp or the other.

She went upstairs to the second floor. She'd been up here once as a room mother on a field trip, but never on her own. To the right of the wide, well-worn oak stairs was a series of "period" rooms that a visitor could walk through. A late-Victorian bedroom, parlor, and kitchen. She liked the way the velvet-roped path led through the center of the rooms, rather than having to view them from the doorway, and the Snellen had banned identifying tags on everything. At each doorway was a guide to the room, a little drawing that numbered and described each item on display. That was nice. Much more realistic and less "museum-y." Since there were no other visitors, she had the imaginary house to herself. Perhaps it was the recent experience of trying to imagine herself in an earlier time, perhaps not, but she found herself pretending this was a real home.

The bedroom had masses of little things to dust—pictures,

paper flowers, vases, lamps with hideous ruffled and fringed shades. The parlor was much the same and crammed with furniture that would have been waxed at least weekly by a house-proud Victorian wife. Or her maid, Jane thought. And the lady of a house like this one would probably seldom have entered the kitchen. Some poor cook had to cope with the huge, sullen oven with all the ornamental bits to collect grease, the cold granite sinks, the pump for water, the huge, heavy bowls and cooking pans.

How did they survive such a life? Jane wondered. She'd have to make a point of remembering this display the next time she became cranky about car pools, computer glitches, and vacuum-cleaner ailments.

Did people who made their living in the museum business ever just roam around and let their imaginations run riot? Or did they come to regard the place in a strictly business sense, losing sight of the forest with concern for the trees? Had Regina Palmer ever stood here pretending this was her kitchen and she was the woman who had to haul the dirty dishwater out the back door and dump it next to the kitchen garden? Had she imagined sleeping in that high bed and having to find the little steps in order to climb down to use the chamber pot at night? Or had Regina, out of necessity and perhaps inclination, been more concerned with tour schedules, salary increments, accounting procedures, professional publications, and the quest to snag touring exhibits?

Without having met Regina, Jane couldn't guess. But she certainly couldn't imagine Derek Delano entering into a sort of fugue state and truly appreciating the sense of another time that a well-planned museum could produce. The man had struck her as having imagination only when it came to his sexual fantasies.

She had left the room displays and was wandering aimlessly down the hall to the next room when she heard a strange noise. A faint voice. Tapping. She glanced around, unable to determine where it was coming from. She continued down the hall, but the sound grew fainter. Turning, she headed for the stairs. Yes, it was coming from above. She climbed the stairs cautiously, listening.

Finally, she located the source of the sporadic sounds. A heavy door just beyond the third-floor landing. And the voice was Babs's. She tried the door, but it was locked.

"Who is that?" Babs called out.

"It's me, Jane. The door's locked."

"Then get the key," Babs said sharply.

Jane dashed down the stairs and examined the board on which the keys hung, but there were dozens of them. There was no one in the hallway to the staff offices, not even the police officer, so she went into the boardroom. It was mobbed. Caspar Snellen was trying awkwardly to comfort Georgia, who was sobbing. Whitney Abbot was tinkering with the computer. Mel was there, too, speaking to Lisa. Jumper, Sharlene, and Shelley were standing around the coffee machine, shaking their heads in despair.

Everybody turned at Jane's entrance.

"Babs McDonald is locked in a room on the third floor," she said. "And I don't know which key I need to get her out."

"Oh, my God!" Lisa exclaimed, heading for the door and colliding with Sharlene, who was headed in the same direction.

"Just give me the key," Mel said. "I'll go. Jane, you come with me."

When they finally found the right key and rushed back upstairs, they discovered that the room Babs was locked in was a dark closet. She all but fell out. "I hate dark places," she said, maintaining a shaky dignity.

"What happened? Are you all right?" Mel demanded.

"Of course I'm all right. I came up here to look in the file cabinet that's kept in that horrible closet. I heard footsteps, but didn't think much about it until the door slammed shut. And even then I wasn't especially disconcerted until the light burned out."

"Do you have any idea who it was?" Mel asked.

"None. I had my back turned to the door."

"How long have you been in there?" Jane asked.

Babs looked at her watch, then held it up to her ear before looking at it again. "My goodness. Only about fifteen minutes. But it seemed much longer."

"Why would somebody lock you in the closet?" Jane wondered.

"As a warning, apparently. Thank goodness you were around to hear me."

"A warning of what?" Mel said.

Babs stared at him for a long moment, then replied, "I haven't the faintest idea."

Chapter 20

"**Jane, what in** the world were you doing up there?" Shelley asked as they drove home.

"Just trying to get my thoughts in order."

"It's a good thing you didn't get yourself and your thoughts locked in a closet."

"If Babs is right, I wouldn't have been anyway," Jane said, cringing as Shelley's van whispered by a parked car. She could almost hear the paint on both vehicles gasping at the near miss. As much as she loved and admired Shelley, the way Shelley drove always left her gibbering with terror.

She drew a deep breath and continued. "Babs said she'd been locked in there as a warning."

"A warning about what?"

"Not to talk about something, presumably. But that's as far as she'd go. Either she really doesn't know what she was being warned off or she's making a convincing show of not knowing."

"Which wouldn't surprise me," Shelley said. "I think Babs

McDonald could have persuaded Newt to head up the Democratic National Committee if she'd set her mind to it. But just the same, if she has some idea, I'll bet she's told the police."

"Who aren't going to tell us," Jane said glumly.

"She really was indignant about the way Lisa and Sharlene kept fussing over her," Shelley said.

"It's probably the only time they've treated her like a fragile little old lady."

Shelley executed an almost perfect right-angle turn into the parking lot of the neighborhood post office. "I have to mail some underwear," she said. "Paul's sister, Constanza, stayed with us for a couple days and left a bra, which she wants mailed. Don't you think if you left a trail of lingerie, you'd keep quiet and hope nobody noticed? And it's a tatty, ragged old thing nobody in their right mind would claim."

It was an awfully big box and, knowing Shelley, Jane suspected the item had been washed, ironed, and stuffed into bosom shape with elegant tissue. Shelley knew how to be nasty in the classiest ways. She came back to the car looking smug, which confirmed Jane's thoughts.

"Putting Babs's incarceration aside for a minute, I have some gossip you'll like," Jane said. She told Shelley about her conversation with Sharlene.

"He forgot the bathrooms? A hoity-toity architect left out the potties?" Shelley exclaimed delightedly. "He's probably so inhuman he doesn't use them himself."

"I admit he's kind of a cold fish," Jane said, "but I think you hated him on sight. Why?"

Shelley shrugged and honked at an inoffensive man trying

to cut in on her traffic lane. "I don't know. Maybe he reminds me of somebody, or maybe it's just instinct."

"You think he's the murderer?"

"I think it's possible. Or at least not *im*possible."

"Then here's the rest of what Sharlene said. She mentioned that he'd referred to the incident again yesterday afternoon when he came to the museum to pick up something."

"He was at the Snellen yesterday? When Derek was killed?"

"Good God, Shelley! Keep your eyes on the road! We don't know when Derek was killed, but if it was yesterday, your favorite suspect is still a suspect."

"And he was there today when Babs was locked in the closet," Shelley said.

"So, it appears, was everyone else," Jane reminded her. "What were Georgia and Caspar doing there?"

"I'm not sure. I got the impression someone had called and told Georgia about Derek and she had brought Caspar along with her to find out what was going on."

"Was she genuinely upset, do you think?"

Shelley nodded. "I think she was. But still careful not to cry off her mascara and eyeliner. Probably five on a scale of ten."

"So it all could have been for show?" Jane asked. "What about Lisa? I thought she'd gone home for the day."

"Sharlene called her at my urging," Shelley said. "The director and acting director were dead, Babs was missing, and Jumper hadn't arrived yet. I figured Lisa was the logical person to represent the museum. And it didn't seem the kind of thing she should learn about on the evening news."

"And were they all there in time to have locked Babs up?"

"Probably. I just thought Babs was in the bathroom or using the phone or something, so I didn't have any reason to pay attention to when people arrived," Shelley said. "There was a police officer outside the front door letting people in, but once they were inside, I don't imagine there was anyone watching just where they went. Mind if I stop at the grocery store?"

"Nope. I need to make a hit-and-run stop, too."

Jane had a longing for chili and crackers, but that was merely a reflection of her longing for it to be fall. She dashed through the store and grabbed hamburger patties, baked beans, a head of lettuce, some chips, and—after some mental agonizing—hamburger buns. She probably had the remains of three packages of buns in various stages from fresh to mildewed beyond recognition, but if she didn't buy some, there wouldn't be any at home. She left Shelley having a conversation with a clerk about coupons that looked like it might become acrimonious.

"She finally saw it my way," Shelley said when she was back in the car.

After Jane arrived at home, she discovered that she did indeed have an unopened bag of hamburger buns, so she put the new ones in the freezer, knowing full well they'd be freezer-burned by the next time she noticed them. She glanced at her watch. It would be a good hour before she had to start dinner. Notes on the refrigerator door indicated that Mike and Katie would both be back by five-thirty, and the sound of her big yellow dog, Willard, tearing up and down the stairs chasing a ball told her that Todd was home.

"Todd, stop letting that dog tear up the carpet!" she bellowed. "I'm going next door."

WAR AND PEAS

"Uh-oh, Willard-billiard, you're in *big* trouble!" Todd's voice drifted down.

Shelley was on the phone and gestured silently at Jane to come in. Jane sat at Shelley's kitchen table and waited patiently while an elaborate car-pool schedule was negotiated. When Shelley got off the phone, she said, "Someday we'll look back on car pools and laugh. Not any day soon, but someday I'll bash you with my walker and cackle, 'Jane, weren't those car pools fun?' "

"And I'll poke you in the ribs with my cane and say, 'If only we could go do some more work for the PTA.' And then the nice young nurses will come give us our meds."

"Yes, and say what dear old things we are."

"I'm feeling sort of old-dearish right now," Jane said. "Overwhelmed and confused."

"Let's sit on the patio, where I can pretend not to hear the phone," Shelley suggested. "Want something to drink?"

"Anything but coffee. I'm caffeined out." Jane wandered outdoors and sat down under the shade of Shelley's picnic-table umbrella. She slipped off her shoes and put her feet up on an empty chair.

When Shelley emerged, she had two clear, iced drinks with her. Jane took a gulp of hers and exclaimed, "What in the world is this!"

"Black-cherry-flavored spring water," Shelley said, taking a cautious sip. "Hmm. I think it's better in theory than for real. It came in such pretty cans, too. Pity."

"Shelley, tell me what we know about this business at the museum. What we really know, not what might be."

"Not much," Shelley admitted. "Two people are dead, the director and the acting director. Somebody is or was looking for something in Regina's office and in the basement. Somebody locked Babs in a closet. That's about it. Oh, and somebody threatened Regina. No, come to think of it, we don't know that for sure. It could have been a joke."

"I don't think so. We'll have to ask Mel about fingerprints on the note. If nobody but Regina and Lisa left prints on it, I think we can assume it was a threat. Nobody goes to the trouble of wearing gloves to write a note that's a joke."

"Okay," Jane said, "let's assume for a minute that the same person is responsible for all of this. I'm not sure that's a legitimate assumption, but it does mean one thing. That the unknown person is intimately involved with the museum."

"Because—?"

"Because he—or she—knew there would be an opportunity to shoot Regina for real in the midst of the fake shooting. Because he knows or thinks there's something valuable or threatening in Regina's office and in the basement. Unless he was familiar with the museum, he wouldn't even know there was a basement, much less be able to lure Derek down there."

"Maybe Derek wasn't lured," Shelley said, taking another sip of her drink. "Maybe he went down for some reason of his own and caught someone who shouldn't have been there."

"Possibly. But why would he have gone down there? The last time anybody saw him, he was stomping off with a box full of résumés to look for another job. Why would he detour to the basement?"

"The only reason I can think of is that he was meeting someone—maybe someone who said they needed to speak to him privately. Anything you say in the staff area seems to echo all over the place."

Jane nodded. "On the surface, this looks like it had to do with the job of director. Regina was the director and was killed; Derek was appointed acting director and he was killed. But that's the end of that chain of reasoning. Nobody else wanted the job."

"Maybe Lisa did, despite saying otherwise," Shelley said without much conviction.

"But she had a good job that she'd done very well. She probably could have gotten a better-paying, more prestigious job in another museum if money and prestige were what she wanted," Jane said.

"That leaves all the people in the file the board is considering," Shelley said. "And presumably none of them knew enough about the museum and the people there to have pulled this off."

They sat in discouraged silence for a few minutes before Shelley said, "As much as it annoys you, let me go back to my favorite suspect for a minute. Suppose Whitney Abbot had made some horrible mistake with the plans, something even more horrible than leaving out bathrooms. And Regina found out—"

Jane rolled her eyes and said, "Go on."

"Well, if he had a reason like that to kill Regina to save his reputation, then Derek could also know about it. Didn't you say that he mentioned something to Jumper about looking through Regina's files?"

"The job-applicant files, yes. But, Shelley, do you really believe Regina would have had a file labeled 'Terrible Architectural Errors?' "

"Okay, okay. It was just a thought."

"Shelley, I don't think it has anything to do with the job."

"Why not?"

"Instinct? A wild guess? All these people are highly qualified, respected professionals who could have gone anywhere. Probably somewhere better in terms of salary and benefits if they'd really wanted to. Even Derek, who's a sexist jerk, is supposed to be well educated and qualified. He could have gotten a job at some place where his contempt of women might not have bothered anyone."

"Like where?" Shelley exclaimed.

Jane grinned. "The Citadel? They must have a military museum. Okay, I'm kidding. My point is, I can't imagine anyone killing someone over the directorship of the Snellen Museum."

"Then why were they killed?" Shelley asked.

"Some help you are!" Jane said. "There are bound to be better reasons. More 'passionate' reasons."

"Jane, I think we're in over our heads. Maybe this is one of those times we should just shut up and let the police figure it out."

"Are you suggesting that a woman who can change a spark plug and hang a bird feeder can't figure out a double murder?" Jane asked.

"I don't think those are really related skills," Shelley replied.

Chapter**21**

Jane went home and started dinner. She fried some bacon, set it aside to drain, and poured a can of pearl onions into a sieve, then into the bottom of a baking dish. A large can of baked beans went on top of the onions, then a drizzle of molasses, and finally the crumbled bacon. She put the baking dish into the oven and cleaned up the top of the molasses jar before putting the lid back on. She'd learned to do that after permanently gluing the tops on three or four bottles. Her baked beans were a nuisance to make, but the kids loved them and she had something of a local reputation on the neighborhood picnic circuit for them.

She dialed Mel's office number, but he wasn't in. She didn't leave a message. He'd call when he got a chance anyway, and it wasn't as if she had anything worthwhile to tell him, nor did she want to openly pump him for information. He'd tell her what he could, when he could. She'd been involved with him in murder investigations before. In fact, that was how she'd met him. Shelley had found a dead cleaning lady in her guest bedroom and Mel had been the detective in charge of the investigation. Back then, he'd thought their interest was merely interference. But Shelley and Jane had solved the case—Mel called it "stumbling onto the solution"—and his attitude had changed slightly.

Though he'd never admit it, they'd helped him a couple of times, and he'd learned that he could share some information with them and trust that they wouldn't go blabbing it around or put themselves in danger—at least, not much danger—by snooping. Jane and Shelley didn't fool themselves into thinking they were better at solving crimes than the police were. They just had a different fix.

The police had all the technical expertise: the fingerprint people, the specialists in blood, fiber, and DNA—the people who could make a case hold up in court. And they had the manpower to check alibis, look into suspects' legal histories, and call on other, far-flung law-enforcement agencies. But they were, of necessity, slow and meticulous, not given to the bizarre flights of imagination that had sometimes led Jane and Shelley in the right direction. While Mel concentrated on evidence, they tended to chew over relationships.

Occasionally they "chewed" them into unrecognizable shreds, Jane thought. This was such a case. Too many relationships, too many people whose real feelings about others were a mystery. And at the heart of this case, Regina Palmer. Jane still had no clear idea of what the woman had been like, and that kept nagging at her. It wasn't just that she'd seen Regina only briefly in life. Jane had the feeling that if she'd met Regina a couple dozen times, she probably wouldn't know much more about what had made her tick. Regina had apparently been a very self-controlled, logical person. A secretive person, but not necessarily in a pejorative sense, as in keeping guilty secrets. Just a person who "kept herself to herself," as Jane's grandmother would have put it.

Nearly everyone spoke of Regina with respect and admiration. There was no question that she had been extremely efficient at her job. But Jane hadn't heard much warmth of feeling expressed. Lisa, as her best friend, spoke of her fondly, and Derek had had some heated negative feelings about her. Yet, taken together, their views didn't seem to make her quite real. Whitney Abbot, a cold fish himself and offended by Shelley's prying, wasn't about to paint a vivid word picture of his fiancée.

Sharlene worshipped Regina, but through an idealistic haze of gratitude. And in spite of her adoration of her boss and the fact that she had kept Regina's appointment diary, Sharlene hadn't seemed to really know her, either. There had been, apparently, an unspoken barrier between them that both women had respected. Sharlene wouldn't have dreamed of prying into Regina's personal life. Even if she'd been curious, doing so would have offended her sense of professional propriety.

As for the others involved with the museum, Caspar made no bones about disliking Regina, but he seemed to dislike anyone who stood in his way. It was an oddly impersonal antipathy based entirely on his thwarted financial expectations. Or was it? Had there perhaps been a genuine spark of antagonism, of clashing personalities, between them? Caspar seemed to rub everyone the wrong way, but nobody had said anything about Regina's feelings toward him. She'd helped Jumper defeat Caspar in the incompetency hearing, but no one had mentioned that she'd ever spoken against him.

Nobody had said, "Boy, was Regina mad!" or, "Regina had really strong feelings about such and such."

Jane couldn't recall that either Jumper or Babs had expressed anything other than a rather impersonal respect for Regina, either. Did any of them ever socialize? Babs, Miss Daisy, and Regina had attended Sharlene's junior-college graduation, but that was a business-type social event. Sharlene was a good, valued employee. But had Regina been the sort of person who would help someone move? Or invite him or her to dinner? Or offer to help pick up a car from the repair shop? If she had been, nobody had indicated that kind of association with her.

Who was Regina Palmer? Jane found herself wondering. What kind of movies had she liked? If she'd rented a video, would it have been the history of the Silk Road or Cheech and Chong or *Wuthering Heights?* If she'd had a pet, would it have been a tank full of exotic, expensive fish, a cage swarming with twittery little birds, or a slightly lame puppy from the pound? Had she liked junk food? Or chocolate? Or had she been a health nut? Had she kept her checkbook balanced? Good chance she had, but maybe she'd been one of those people who was responsible in every area of her life but one. Had she preferred Elvis to Beethoven?

It wasn't that Jane believed that knowing the answers to these questions would solve the mystery of Regina's death. But Regina's character, it seemed, was crucial to the reason for her death, and the questions proved that Jane had no clue to what the woman was about.

She shook her head in frustration as she checked on the progress of the beans. Not hot enough to start the burgers, and besides, Mike and Katie weren't home yet. She lowered the temperature.

Who the hell was Regina? Jane wondered again, frustrated and almost angry at the woman's elusive personality. Was it simply that she'd had no personality? Had she been an automaton? Or a deliberately secretive person? Had she been hiding something so clandestine that she'd tamped down her entire character? A Dreadful Past of some kind? A police record? Surely Mel would have said something if that were the case. Perhaps Regina had been one of those people who pulled themselves up by the bootstraps and didn't want anyone to know about their humble origins.

Or maybe my imagination's run amok, Jane thought wryly.

Since Mike and Katie still hadn't turned up, she began fixing some dip to go with the chips for dinner. Another of her best things—dip. Fortunately, she had a cucumber in the fridge that hadn't started on the road to slime, and there was a fresh block of cream cheese. She seeded the cucumber, cut it and the cream cheese into cubes, tossed them into the food processor with some lemon juice and garlic salt, and let the machine turn them into Food for the Gods.

Mel called after dinner. "I thought you'd want to know that Caspar Snellen has been taken in for questioning," he said, sounding irritated.

"Arrested?"

"Not yet."

"Why?" Jane asked.

"Because his greasy fingerprints are all over that pea-storage thing."

"You're not happy with this, are you?"

There was a long silence before he finally said, "No, I'm not. But I'm not in charge."

"And you're wishing you were," Jane concluded. "Why don't you agree?"

Mel sighed. "A lot of reasons. Partly because he has a story to account for the prints. He says he heard some visitor telling about a fantastic pea that would, if he could find it, revolutionize agriculture. It's such a nutty, Caspar-trying-to-get-something-for-nothing story that I'm inclined to believe him. It's not that I think he *couldn't* have committed the murders. He's very much a suspect in my mind. But I don't think the fingerprints prove anything."

"Mel, I knew about that amazing pea. I should have told you," Jane said. "Couldn't he have been rummaging around down in the basement and Derek interrupted him? He could be vicious when his get-rich-quick schemes are thwarted."

"That's just it, Jane. He is, at heart, a petty criminal. And even the stupidest crooks know you don't leave fingerprints all over the scene of a crime."

"But wasn't trying to steal the pea a crime?"

"Not the way he sees it. He says his great-grandfather developed it, and it's rightly his. He reluctantly includes his sister as a potential beneficiary. Besides, rummaging around in that cabinet isn't a crime that was likely to involve a crime lab and fingerprints. It was just snooping."

"Did he find the pea?"

"Jane! Who cares? Like anybody could grow a fifty- or sixty-year-old pea! It's just another loony idea of his."

Jane didn't want to argue seed viability, especially since she was completely ignorant on the subject—not that such considerations always stopped her—but she said, "Still, did he find the pea?"

"He claims he didn't."

"Good. If that pea exists and if it could grow and if it could be patented, it shouldn't belong to him."

"Given all those *ifs*, I'm not sure you're right, legally. But it doesn't matter. I don't care about the amazing pea—I care about the real murderer being caught. And Rolly's just trying to swirl his cape and show off that he can solve a murder investigation from the privacy of his own bathroom."

"Rolly's the officer in charge? And he's still sick?"

"I was overstating it a bit," Mel admitted.

Jane smiled smugly. He was always accusing her of this sin. But she didn't let her satisfaction creep into her voice. "What about Regina's death? How does Rolly figure that?"

"Sheer dislike, frustration, and annoyance on Caspar's part. Regina had, in his view, tricked him out of a fortune that should have been his, and after exhausting all his legal recourses, he just went berserk and killed her out of spite. I don't buy it. Caspar Snellen is a coward. His method of operation is annoying lawsuits. He'd brought at least a dozen of them against various people in the last ten years and collected rather nicely. He's one of those people who deliberately trip on escalators and then sue the hell out of the department store."

"You're kidding!"

"He never wins, legally. Because the stores always settle rather than going to the trouble and expense of going to court. He's done well at it. Fifty grand here, seventy-five there."

"Doesn't sound like a man who would shoot a woman

out of spite," Jane said. "If he's that good at the legal she-nanigans, he could have exercised his spite by inundating the museum, and Regina, with frivolous suits."

"That's my thinking, too," Mel said. "I don't discount the fact that he could kill. But not for the motives Rolly's come up with. Either the motives are wrong or the suspect is."

"Or both," Jane said.

"Most likely both," Mel agreed. "Oh, something else you're sure to ask me about sooner or later—Regina's will. She left almost everything to Lisa Quigley. The house they lived in, some stocks and bonds."

"When was it written?" Jane asked.

"About a year or so ago," Mel said.

"Nothing to her family?"

"Nope," Mel replied. "She was an only child, parents both dead. There is an aunt and uncle who seem to be pretty well off in their own right. There were a few other bequests, too. The public television station, the Salvation Army."

"Nothing to the museum?"

"No, but the will was written after Daisy Snellen died. She knew the museum had already been extremely generously endowed."

"That makes sense," Jane said. "How much of an estate are we talking about?"

"About two hundred thousand, plus the house. Uh-ho, I'm being paged. Talk to you later."

Chapter**22**

Jane finished cleaning up the kitchen, bellowed at the kids that she was going next door, and went to report in to Shelley about her call from Mel.

"What in the world are you doing?" Jane asked. Shelley had covered her kitchen table with a piece of plastic and had some tools, brushes, rags, bottles, and a bunch of tarnished silver serving pieces laid out.

"I'm polishing silver. For the last time ever!" she exclaimed. "Paul's mother is a great believer in silver, as you know. I've never figured out if it's an especially Polish thing or just her private obsession, but she keeps giving me these things and I'm expected to keep them polished and on display at all times. But I've had one of those Life-Changing Revelations. She called this afternoon when she got home from a trip and told me that her hip is still giving her trouble and she's decided she's not ever going on a plane again and we'll have to visit her instead. That scenario has its drawbacks, but on the other hand, she'd never know that

I've cleaned this stuff for the last time, wrapped it in airtight plastic, and put it away. So what do you want to work on?"

"Shelley, your house is going to look empty without all this."

"Yes! Won't it be wonderful?"

"Give me a platter. I'm good with platters. Mel just called. We were right about someone overhearing the elderly gentleman's discussion with Sharlene about the Little Beauty pea. It was Caspar and his fingerprints were all over the pea-bin drawers."

Shelley handed Jane a platter, a rag, and a bottle of silver polish. "Do the police think he killed Derek?"

"Mel doesn't. Rolly, who's the officer in charge, does. Mel isn't happy. They haven't arrested Caspar yet, but have him in for questioning." Jane went on to recount her conversation with Mel as best she could remember it, including Caspar's skills at initiating frivolous but profitable lawsuits.

Shelley put a tiny buffing pad on a miniature electric drill, smeared the pad with silver polish, and plugged in the drill, but didn't turn it on yet. "I'm inclined to agree with Mel," she said thoughtfully. "It seems to me that a person who knows how to use and abuse the legal system as well as Caspar can would be unlikely to simply ignore it and resort to violence. Not that Caspar couldn't be driven to violence by something, but not, I think, by the faint possibility of those peas being able to grow and him being able to someday make money on them."

"I agree, but if he were furtively rummaging around in the pea bin and Derek took him by surprise—? Remember,

Derek was already very angry over his conversation with Jumper. Derek might have gotten very nasty with him."

Shelley turned on the little drill and applied the whirling buffer pad to some elaborate scrollwork on a serving fork. "Yes, but what was Derek doing down there?"

"Good question. I have no idea."

"I can't think of any reason, either, except that somebody asked to meet him down there. And that suggests a plan, not an accidental meeting. So if you eliminate the element of surprise, what possible reason would Caspar have for killing Derek?"

"And Regina," Jane added.

"Yes, and Regina. But for the moment, let's consider Derek's murder alone. We don't even know when Caspar was in the basement, do we? He might well have gotten his hands all over the pea bin any time this week. In fact, he was probably the one who messed things up down there a couple days ago. Before Derek was killed."

Shelley got up and rinsed the silver polish off the fork at the sink and held up the result proudly. "Are you impressed?" she asked.

"Enormously," Jane said dryly. "How come you get a power tool, even if it is a wimpy little one, and I'm the slave labor with the rag and the toothbrush?"

"I think it's just because Life Isn't Fair."

"Mel says Caspar's being very defensive about the pea thing," Jane went on. "He's claiming he has every right to try to find and develop it since it was originally grown by his great-grandfather. I guess the legality of that would depend on Auguste's will. But the fact is, Caspar has convinced himself of it. All the more reason to discount the theory of Guilty Surprise."

"So if we eliminate Caspar and assume someone asked Derek to meet them down in the basement, who have we got?"

"Practically anyone," Jane said.

Shelley was working on another serving fork. "Isn't it most likely it was a spur-of-the-moment thing having to do with the nasty things he'd just said to Jumper? Who did he go after? Babs, Georgia, and Jumper himself."

"Right. Plus a crack about Regina and one about Jumper's friend the anchorwoman."

"I think we can probably eliminate the anchorwoman," Shelley said with a smile. "And Regina was dead by then."

"All he said about Jumper was that he dressed funny— and Jumper *does* dress funny. Apparently it's deliberate. Besides, it's inconceivable that anyone would kill somebody because of a comment about their wardrobe."

"Right. Otherwise that guy who does the Worst Dressed List would have been blown away years ago. So that leaves Babs and Georgia, both of whom were around and could have heard what Derek said."

"Yes, and Babs explained to us what he meant about her killing her husband."

Shelley looked up and turned off the drill. "Actually, Babs told us what she wanted us to know. It was certainly convincing and probably the truth, but—well, what if it wasn't, Jane? What if it was just her sheer force of personality that convinced us?"

Jane thought for a minute. "But her story does match what

Sharlene told us about the newspaper article. Once you discount Sharlene's romanticism.''

''Okay, that's right. So that leaves us with Georgia, who's an ideal suspect.''

''Uh-huh. She could have killed Derek because he'd dumped her—or was getting ready to. The Lover Scorned. And she must have known she was under a cloud over fudging the fund-raising. And if she had confided in Derek about some other funny-money stunts, then heard him shooting off his mouth—well—''

''And she's a suspect in Regina's death as well. For much the same financial reasons.'' Shelley turned the serving fork around to work on the other end. ''You know, there's another possibility, if, in fact, Derek's death is related to what he said to Jumper.''

''Let me guess. Whitney Abbot.''

''Listen, Jane, it's possible. He'd lost his fiancée and then overheard a slimeball calling her names and commenting on her sexual preferences. He'd be justified in being real damned angry.''

Jane got up to rinse off the platter she'd been working on. ''You're going to have to do the fancy stuff around the edges,'' she said, reaching for a dishtowel to dry the piece. ''Okay, I'll give you the point that Whitney would have found Derek's comments offensive if he heard them, or heard about them. The problem with that theory is Regina's death. I find it hard enough to believe that one of the people at the museum is a murderer, and impossible to consider that two people are. If Whitney killed Derek, don't we have to assume he killed Regina, too? And if he killed Regina for some reason of his own, he'd hardly compound the crime by bumping off someone who criticized her."

"That's a bit baroque, but I think I see what you mean."

"Oh, I almost forgot the rest. About Regina's will. It was made a year or so ago. She left something to a couple charities, including the local public television station—which is the first thing I've heard about her that makes me really like her—and the rest, including the house she and Lisa shared, to Lisa."

"How much was her estate?" Shelley asked.

"Mel said about two hundred thousand dollars, plus the house, whatever that's worth. Or more likely the equity in the house."

"Did she own it herself or did she leave Lisa her joint share?"

"I didn't think to ask."

"Two hundred thousand," Shelley mused. "A nice amount of money. Even once the taxes are paid on it. But not enough to kill your best friend for, especially when you have a good job yourself."

"Money's a good motive, though," Jane said doubtfully. "And Regina would probably have done a new will after she married. What kind of house did they live in?"

"I don't know, but I had the impression they lived quite close to the museum, and there aren't any outstandingly valuable properties in that neighborhood that I know of."

"I have the feeling we're looking at this all wrong," Jane said, selecting a silver bowl with very simple, easily cleanable lines. "As if we're asking the wrong questions of ourselves."

"What do you mean?"

"Well, we're asking who could have heard what. Who could have been where? But maybe the question is simple: who's better off now than before Regina and Derek died?"

"So who is?"

"Maybe it really does have to do with the directorship in one way or another," Jane said. "Somebody's going to have a new job as director—although I doubt that's a consideration unless some unknown job applicant decided to lurk around, explore the entire museum, and create a position by killing off people. The other possibility—and this one is real—is that there's something only the director and the assistant director knew that was highly dangerous to someone."

"But what could they have known that nobody else did?" Shelley asked. "It's not as if they were chummy. In fact, they seemed to barely get along. Derek wanted Regina's job; Regina regretted having recommended him as assistant. If Regina knew something to someone's detriment, she'd be much more likely to tell Lisa, who's her friend, or Jumper, who's the museum's lawyer, or Whitney, who's her fiancé. In fact, she'd probably have confided in Babs or even Sharlene before she'd tell Derek an important secret. And Derek, if he revealed anything, might have revealed it to Georgia, although I doubt even that."

Jane nodded. "Funny. The only person you didn't mention was Caspar."

Shelley looked surprised. "That's true. But we're assuming that this secret, whatever it might have been, was told voluntarily. Caspar's a great one for snooping around and eavesdropping. That's how he knew about the Little Beauty pea. But to go back to your question about who's better off now. Nobody."

Jane said, "I guess you're right. Sharlene's lost a good boss. Lisa's lost a best friend. Jumper and Babs have lost their director and will have to spend a lot of time and effort finding a replacement."

Shelley added, "Georgia's lost a lover. Whitney's lost a fiancée. And Caspar had already lost a fortune he thought was half his, but the murders won't change that."

"And Regina and Derek lost everything," Jane said quietly.

Chapter**23**

Jane and Shelley arrived at the museum early the next morning, determined to make up for lost time. They found a stranger in the boardroom, a gaunt, pale individual who looked alarmingly like the late Andy Warhol. He was seated at the center table with a lot of file folders spread around him.

"Can I help you ladies?" he asked, glaring at them as if they'd broken in and were planning to steal his files.

Shelley introduced herself and Jane and explained that they were the volunteers entering information in the database preparatory to the move to the new facilities.

As she spoke, his face relaxed. "I'm sorry if I sounded rude. It's just that I had an ugly moment with some gawkers outside when I arrived. There was an article about Derek in this morning's paper, and this couple, whom I assume to be badly disguised reporters, made no bones about the fact that they wanted to get in to pry."

"And you are—?" Jane asked.

He shook her hand. "I'm Eli Bascomb." He said it as if they should recognize his name, then added, "The accountant."

"I thought you were in Alaska or some place," Jane said.

"I was. Due back next week anyway, and my brother's kids were driving me crazy. So I used my frequent-flyer miles and came back for the board meeting today."

"There's a board meeting today?" Jane said, thinking irritably that she'd lose even more time at the computer.

He glanced at his watch. "In about an hour."

Sharlene bustled into the room with a stack of papers. "You're early, Jane. Hi, Shelley. Eli, have you got your papers ready for the board packet?"

"Yes, right here."

Sharlene fired up the copier and busied herself making copies and collating them into neat piles. Bascomb rummaged around in his files. Shelley stashed her purse and collected her blank forms and clipboard. Somewhere in the hall outside, a radio was turned on and the sounds of "Bad, Bad Leroy Brown" filled the air.

Jane switched on the computer and while it was booting up, she set her purse next to Heidi on the shelf. As she did so, she inadvertently unbalanced the stuffed cat, which tumbled off the shelf. She made a quick grab and caught it as it fell. "Poor Heidi," she said quietly. She'd caught it upside down and turned it upright gently, hoping the fragile old thing hadn't suffered any damage.

Then she stood and stared into space for a long minute, her mind racing.

Shelley was just leaving the room. Jane spun around and said, "Shelley, wait up. I need to have a quick word with you."

Holding the cat carefully, she all but pushed Shelley out the door.

"What is it?" Shelley asked.

"Shh. Come with me," Jane said.

They left the staff area, went through the central hallway, and found a quiet place in a corner of a deserted display room. Keeping her voice down, Jane said, "Look at the bottom of the cat."

"I'd just as soon not," Shelley replied.

"No, the wooden thingy it's mounted on," Jane said, turning Heidi over.

On the bottom of the plaquelike board on which the cat was mounted, there was a square of a different wood set in level with the base. A yellowed paper was stuck down to the insert and was tattered around the edges. There were a few letters of faded writing on it.

"What?" Shelley asked.

"It's a little door," Jane said. "An opening. And listen."

She shook the cat gently. There was a faint, muffled rattling sound.

"Ick. Its stuffing has lumped up," Shelley said. Then her eyes widened and she said, "Or—"

"Or it's hollow and stuffed with something that rattles," Jane said. "Can you read what's on the paper?"

Shelley leaned over and looked closely. "A pea formula. Just like on the bins in the basement."

They stared at each other for a minute. Jane said, "The cat's name is Heidi."

"Heidi," Shelley said. "Or 'hidey'?"

"Exactly. And somebody told us Auguste Snellen was a secretive man about his pea crosses."

"Jane, do you think the Little Beauty peas are inside this cat?"

"I don't know, but it could be. Jot down the numbers on the paper and we'll check them against that ledger."

"When did Auguste die?" Shelley asked.

"Babs told us, but I don't remember exactly what she said. Sometimes in the nineteen-thirties."

"Possibly just after receiving the letter from Arkansas about the way Little Beauty helped the other crops grow," Shelley whispered. "Maybe he saw the potential, intended to pursue it, and hid the peas in the stuffed cat. But maybe he died before he could start a new batch of them for experimentation. Shake it again."

Jane did so. "It sounds like it could be peas."

They heard footsteps. Shelley hurriedly placed her forms on the upside-down base of the stuffed cat as if it were a temporary desk surface and said in a normal tone of voice, "Okay, I'll do that room next. I've already got a few items listed here, you see, but I'll wait to give them to you until I have the whole room inventoried."

The lady who ran the gift shop poked her head around the display board they were lurking behind. "You gave me a start. I didn't know anyone was in here. You haven't seen a pair of sunglasses, have you? I put them down somewhere yesterday and can't remember where."

Jane smiled. "I haven't noticed them. I'll keep an eye out, though."

"Thanks, dear," the gift-shop lady said, wandering away.

"What do we do now?" Shelley whispered.

"I think we better just put the cat back on the shelf in the boardroom for now," Jane said. "I'm the only one who has any interest in it. We'll sneak it out later and see what's really inside. Meanwhile, I'll check out this number in the ledger."

"If it's the same number as the Little Beauty, I guess we ought to give it to the police to safeguard until the murders are solved. Then the museum and Caspar can sort out who the peas actually belong to." Shelley stopped speaking and smiled wickedly. "Please, Jane, oh, please, *please* let me be there when you hand a stuffed cat over to Mel. It'll be the highlight of my life."

Jane set the cat back upright and started giggling. "I don't know if our relationship can withstand my turning in a stuffed cat for custody."

Jane went back to the boardroom, trying to carry the cat as if she were mildly perplexed to find it in her possession. She put it back on the shelf, gave it a friendly pat, and pretended to fix her attention on the computer while actually looking around to see where she'd put the old pea ledger. She spotted it under a stack of inventory forms, but didn't risk looking into it.

Sharlene had finished her collating and was setting out tidy piles of paperwork around the board table. Eli Bascomb had put most of his file folders back in his briefcase and was writing on a notepad. Jane would have loved to tell Sharlene what she and Shelley had discovered, but Eli was an unknown factor and she knew better than to say anything until the cat was safely hidden away. Besides, she and Shelley might be jumping to a very silly conclusion and could discover that Heidi was only hiding some clumped-up cotton batting or sawdust. Better that no one else know.

Lisa came into the room just then. Speaking to Sharlene,

she said, "I've gotten word from the police that we can bury Regina tomorrow. I'm running her things over to the funeral home now. If you'd call the paper for me to see that a notice is placed, and let her aunt and uncle know, we can both be done in time for the board meeting."

Eli Bascomb followed Lisa out, telling her how shocked he'd been at the news of Regina's death. Sharlene finished arranging the paperwork and left as well.

Jane focused on the computer, forcing herself to tune out the activities around her. The gift-shop lady came in, made copies of something to add to the packets, and left. Babs followed a few minutes later and repeated the process and departed, muttering to herself about something she'd left in the car.

Caspar, having apparently avoided arrest so far, came in next. Jane had the urge to grab Heidi and the ledger and clutch them to her, but managed to pretend not even to notice him. He sat down at the table and started rummaging through a board packet. Jane resisted the urge to run and tattle on him, only because it would have left the cat and the book unprotected. He flapped pages around and snorted to himself.

Babs returned shortly and said, "What are you doing here, Caspar?"

"Board meetings are open to the public, aren't they?"

"Don't tell me you are grouping yourself with 'the public'?" she said sarcastically.

"Somebody's got to keep an eye on you people," he said too loudly. "Sneaking around here killing each other off and trying to shove the blame on me."

"Not very successfully, it appears," she drawled.

WAR AND PEAS

Jumper entered the boardroom before Casper could come up with a reply. Jumper was clothed today in normal clothing, which still managed to look like a costume on him—a dark, three-piece suit, a navy-and-red striped tie, and a white-on-white shirt. His long hair was pulled back in a ponytail.

"Hey, it's a suit!" Caspar said nastily.

"Just for you, Caspar," Jumper said wearily. "Come to snoop on the board meeting?" Not expecting an answer, Jumper sat down and started glancing through the pile of papers Sharlene had prepared.

"What a snotty kid you are," Caspar said. "How you ever got a law degree is a mystery to me. Come to think of it, I might just take a little time and investigate your credentials."

"Oh, give it a rest, Caspar," Jumper said disgustedly.

Babs appeared with Eli Bascomb in tow. "Oh, Jumper, I'm glad you're here," she said. "Eli and I were just discussing a change in the federal withholding and I wanted to consult with you on it. We have a new option on how to compute . . ."

They went into a huddle, ignoring Caspar entirely.

Lisa returned a few minutes later, chatting in low tones with Whitney Abbot. Jane caught a few words about music selections and assumed they were finalizing the plans for Regina's funeral. Both the architect and the publicity director appeared to be entirely unaware of or uninterested in Casper's presence. Jane glanced at him. He was looking around, trying to catch someone's eye, hoping for a fight, it seemed.

Shelley came into the room with a wad of paperwork and said, "Oh, I'm sorry. Are you having a meeting?"

"We're about to," Babs said, "but please stay. In fact, I think it would be nice if you and Jane were present."

Shelley glanced at Jane questioningly, and Jane shrugged her shoulders in ignorance.

An elderly man Jane had never seen before joined the group a minute later, and Babs, Jumper, Lisa, and Whitney greeted him warmly. It seemed, from what they said, that he was one of the honorary members of the board.

Shelley had sidled over to where Jane was and pulled up a chair. "What's going on?" she hissed.

"Board meeting. That's all I know," Jane whispered back.

The room was getting crowded, so Jane turned off the computer and she and Shelley moved their chairs into the corner to make it easier for the others to move around the table. Babs rose and looked out into the hall. "Sharlene? We're about to start. Is Georgia attending the meeting?"

"Yes, she's in the bathroom," Sharlene said, rushing in with her steno pad.

Georgia trailed along a few minutes later, looking downright haggard. There wasn't a chair left at the table and she stood and glared at her brother for a second.

"I'm entitled to be here!" he said defensively.

"You're not allowed to sit in my chair, though. Move it," she said harshly.

Caspar looked like he was going to argue the point, but he changed his mind and got up to lounge against the copying machine, sulking.

Babs glanced at her watch and stood up at the head of the table. "The meeting of the board of the Snellen Museum is called to order," she said crisply.

"Move to dispense with the reading of the minutes," Jumper said automatically.

"Second," Eli Bascomb said.

"Objections?" Babs asked. "Passed. Our first order of business is my report on hiring a new director. I'm very glad to say I believe I've found a perfect candidate."

"Already?" Georgia said.

Jane and Shelley exchanged surprised looks.

Babs nodded. "The candidate is within one credit of obtaining the necessary degree, so I'm recommending appointment as acting director, with the permanent appointment to be made upon completion of the remaining credit. The candidate has a comprehensive grasp of the workings of this museum and staff and a superlative employment record. Sharlene, would you be interested in the job?"

There was a stunned silence, then the sounds of Sharlene's steno pad and pen hitting the floor. "Me? There must be some mistake—"

"No, dear. The only mistake was Regina's not telling me how close you were to completing your degree."

"But that can't be right," Sharlene said. "I was just taking the courses Ms. Palmer suggested—"

"Believe me, I've checked this out very thoroughly," Babs said. "You're lacking only one history course. Now, will you accept the job?"

"I—I—" Sharlene glanced around the table as if waiting for someone to tell her the answer.

Jumper Cable, who'd obviously known about this in advance, grinned at her and nodded.

"Yes—yes, I will," she said, blushing furiously.

"Do I hear a motion?" Babs asked.

Chapter**24**

Jane pretty much tuned out the rest of the board meeting. She'd been surprised and pleased for Sharlene at first, but almost immediately a nasty suspicion had pushed its way into her mind and refused to be dislodged.

Was Sharlene really so astonished to learn that she was within one semester of being qualified to be the director of the Snellen? Could anyone have taken all those years and years of night-school courses and never once wondered what they added up to? Had she never seen her own transcript? Never looked at the course catalog and realized she was close to getting a degree? Even as sweet and obedient as Sharlene was, had she never questioned why Regina was choosing the courses she did?

Sweet. Sharlene was sweet. But there was a core of toughness in her, too. She'd stuck out a demanding job for many, many years. She'd taken a great many classes, not all of which could have been interesting to her, and done well in all of them. And she'd done the same with her job. No one had ever suggested having any problems with her. It wasn't easy creating that kind of persona—the perfect secretary, on top of everything, producing perfect board packets, knowing how everything from the coffeemaker to the laser printer worked, making sure all phone calls were returned, taking care of dozens of disparate little chores. That took real strength. She appeared to be fluffy, but under the fluff there had to be a core of steel.

Jane hated suspecting Sharlene of anything wicked. But the fact was, somebody had cleared a path for her to leap from secretary to director. And who was more likely, in a purely logical sense, to do that than Sharlene herself—the clear beneficiary of those deaths?

Trying to shake off the thought, Jane studied the others in the room. Unless there was a nearly invisible maniac on the loose who was an unknown factor, one of these people had killed two of their own group. Yet it looked like a handful of other groups Jane had been part of—PTA boards, the church fund-raising council. Good, generous people who gave their time and energies to the boring details of keeping a valuable organization running.

They were discussing a traveling exhibit that might be available to them at the time the new museum would open, but which had to be committed to now. Whitney was being questioned about the building schedule, possible glitches in the timing. Jumper was being questioned as to the financial and legal liabilities if the building was not one hundred percent completed when the exhibit arrived. There was serious talk about security, insurance, promotion, and parking facilities. Everyone at the table appeared to be giving his or her full attention to the matter.

Nevertheless, one of those intense, committed individuals was a coldblooded killer.

Eli Bascomb was out of the running. Babs had gotten in touch with him in Alaska, so he was presumably too far away to have been zipping back and forth. And the elderly honorary board member wasn't a likely candidate, either, as Jane had never laid eyes on him at the museum and it was hard to imagine him having the strength or stealth to lurk around without being spotted.

But what of the rest? Jumper was bright and charming, but had an obviously eccentric streak. Babs, too, had a strong personality and her own set of morals. She had admitted killing her husband and made clear she had no regret whatsoever. Lisa had taken on a whole new professional field that didn't particularly interest her, but had done it because it was the sensible thing—and had done it well. That showed strength of character and determination.

So did Whitney's presence today. He was apparently giving his full attention and considerable expertise to the discussion of the traveling-exhibit and building-completion dates while his fiancée lay in a coffin at the funeral home. That couldn't be easy.

Even Georgia, more recently bereaved, was participating in the discussion, asking intelligent and pointed questions. Only Caspar Snellen, surly and wary, leaning against the copy machine and glaring at all of them, *looked* like a murder suspect. But he was basically a coward, hiding behind the law and lawyers to work his many nasty little schemes. Still, a coward could be vicious when cornered. Had Regina cornered him in some way the rest of them knew nothing about? If that were true, why did Derek have to die, too?

WAR AND PEAS

Jane's mind kept coming back to Derek's outburst in this very room. He'd slung around a lot of hateful accusations. Anyone might have heard them. Jane was certain that had led to his death. But perhaps it was what he *hadn't* said. Something that the murderer knew or feared that Derek might say next, rather than what he'd already said? That was a fertile field for speculation. Derek had shown that he could go out of control and blab without restraint. Perhaps someone feared that he'd take up where he left off and had to stop him before he could reveal any more secrets.

There were no more revelations at the board meeting, and it broke up without incident forty-five minutes after starting. The replacement-of-board-member item on the agenda had evidently been postponed. Babs adjourned the meeting as efficiently and briskly as she had convened and conducted it, asking Sharlene to stay for a moment. The others trailed out in twos and threes. Only Jumper, Sharlene, and Babs remained. Babs explained to Sharlene that since it was already Thursday and the museum would be closed the next afternoon for Regina's funeral, Sharlene's appointment as acting director would become official the following Monday. Eli had suggested this for the sake of the bookkeeping, since Sharlene's salary was about to undergo a significant increase.

Shelley took a fresh supply of forms and subtly tapped her ear, instructing Jane to eavesdrop—an instruction Jane hardly needed. As the computer booted up and Jane prepared to go back to work, Babs was suggesting that Sharlene might spend some of the day rearranging Regina's office— now Sharlene's—to her satisfaction.

"And we'll need a new secretary," Babs said. "I'm afraid

we'll never find another one as good as you. Do you want me to help you find someone?"

Sharlene thought for a minute. "There was a woman in one of the classes I took early on who was really good. We've sort of kept in touch and I think she might be willing to take the job. Let me contact her first."

Jane cringed inwardly. That almost sounded like Sharlene had thought this out in advance.

"Uh—Sharlene," Jumper said, "I wonder if—that is—how about a celebration lunch? You and me, I mean," he added.

Jane could almost *hear* Sharlene blush. "Oh, well—yes. That would be nice."

When she'd gone, Jumper said to Babs, "Would you like to come along with us?"

Babs laughed. "No, I would not! I'm much too old to enjoy being the patient observer of Love's Awakening."

Jumper stuttered something that was almost words.

"Or even Sex's Awakening," Babs went on with a chuckle. Then she said, more seriously, "Not that sex isn't a great thing, if it keeps in its proper place. But people like Derek seem to fail miserably in that area. Everything was sex to him. Most of us get sex mixed in a bit with all the other passions, but Derek had it backward."

"I'm not sure I understand that," Jumper said.

"And I'm not sure I can explain it," Babs said. "But look at the passions we're all subject to—ambition, for example. Ambition can be overwhelming. A man can appear to give up everything for his own advancement, but beneath it all, there's always an element of sex. He wants to be rich, successful, revered—and he also wants other men to envy him and women to desire him. Derek's ambition was backward.

He thought he could get what he wanted by being sexy. Oh, well, so much for philosophy. You better go make your lunch reservations."

Jane heard papers rustling as Jumper gathered up his things and left. She sat staring blindly at the computer screen. Babs said good-bye to her, and Jane, preoccupied, mumbled a polite farewell.

Sex, she thought. They'd dismissed sex. Oh, she and Shelley had speculated a bit about Whitney and Regina's relationship and complained about Derek's sleazeball attitudes, but they really hadn't taken sex seriously as a motive. Maybe it was the museum atmosphere that made it seem unlikely.

Her thoughts focused on one person and, like dominoes falling in a neat line, everything clicked. It was, as she had suspected, obvious how everything fitted.

"I **don't want** to leave Heidi and I can hardly sneak her out of the building," she told Shelley a few minutes later, when she found her friend critically studying a diorama of a hog-butchering event at the turn of the century—a gruesome favorite of visiting school groups. "So you're going to have to go outside for lunch and call Mel from wherever you won't be overheard. Once he picks up the cat and the ledger, we have to have a private talk with him."

"Jane, what's wrong? You look really frazzled."

"Shelley, I know who did it and why. I'm certain of it. But we can't talk here."

"Who?" Shelley yelped.

Jane whispered in Shelley's ear.

"No, that can't be," Shelley said.

"It can and is. And it was something you said about Whitney and a comment Babs made about sex that brought it all together. We have to get out of here to talk to Mel about it."

Mel accepted the stuffed cat and the ledger with much better grace than Jane had expected. Shelley was severely disappointed. As soon as he'd gone, Sharlene came into the boardroom. "Jane, your friend the detective just asked me to sign a paper releasing Heidi and a book to the police. I was too stunned to even ask why. What's this about?"

Jane shrugged and lied. "I have no idea. Sharlene, I must leave for a couple hours to take my son to the doctor for his college physical. I don't know if I'll be back today. And Shelley's new crown is loose and she has to see the dentist. I didn't want you to worry what had become of us," she finished, picking up her purse and delving into it for car keys.

Mel was already waiting at Jane's house when they arrived. "You were right," he said as Jane led them inside and started the coffeemaker. "The cat is full of peas."

"I wonder if they'll sprout," Shelley said. "And who they belong to."

"As far as I'm concerned, they belong to the museum," Mel said. "That's who released them to me. Jane, Shelley says you have a theory."

"It's more than a theory. I'm certain I'm right."

She talked for a long time, ticking off items on her fingers as she went. Mel and Shelley made no comments until she was done, then asked a few questions and nodded at her answers. Mel paced the kitchen, frowning. "I've got to admit it does account for everything that's happened. But where's the proof? We can't make an arrest on a good guess."

"Well . . ." Jane said hesitantly, "I have an idea about that, too. But it would involve persuading at least one person to put on a good act and take some risks. I think the individual I have in mind would do it. The museum is going to be closed to the public after the funeral tomorrow, but open to the whole staff for an early supper. That would be the time. Here's what I have in mind . . ."

Chapter**25**

Funerals are usually dismal. And Regina's was more upsetting than most. She'd been young, attractive, bright, successful, and facing what would probably have been the best
of what life had to offer when she was cut down. Added to
that, someone among the mourners had caused her death,
and everyone was aware of it. While people had been doing
their jobs and having their meetings at the museum, the
brutal fact of Regina's death had been dampened slightly.
But the funeral itself was a sad and brutal reminder of the
real loss they'd all suffered.

Jane and Shelley joined the other volunteers after the ser-
vice to return to the museum while Regina's intimate friends
and co-workers went to the cemetery. The entry hall had
been set up for a supper. Tables had been brought in and
laid with paper tablecloths and plastic plates and utensils.
Coffee and tea urns steamed; several trays of cold cuts,
cheeses, rolls, and relishes were put out, covered with plastic
wrap that would be removed when everyone arrived. Some-

one, probably the ever-efficient Sharlene, had had the fore-sight to rent several microwave ovens, which were stuffed with casseroles being kept warm.

Finally the funeral limos arrived. Jane had to smile a little as Jumper came in. He was a tweedy professor today, char-coal leather elbow patches and all. The only thing that was missing was a pipe, and she suspected he had one hidden somewhere on his person. Babs and Sharlene were both in tailored gray-and-white dresses, and Lisa, more traditional, wore deepest black. In deliberate contrast, Caspar Snellen, whose bad taste knew no bounds, had on a plaid jacket and a violently pink shirt. At least he'd stayed away from the funeral itself and turned up only for the food afterward.

Whitney Abbot looked exhausted and wrung out, and Georgia Snellen seemed to have aged a decade or so during the week. Jane assumed the older couple who walked in with the cemetery crowd were Regina's aunt and uncle.

When nearly everyone had a plate, Babs took a place near the front door and the room fell silent. "This probably isn't the time for speeches," she said, "but on behalf of the board of directors and Regina's friends and family, I want to thank all of you for being so kind and organizing this event. This is a sad day for all of us, but in a sense, Regina's vision will remain as we move the Snellen into the future."

She spoke for a few more minutes. The words consisted of formal platitudes, but Babs's musical voice made them seem very personal and sincere. After she had finished and sat down, other conversations sprang up, making the entry hall appear to hum.

The board and staff of the museum were seated at two adjoining tables, and as Jane examined something that looked like breaded peppers, Whitney approached Jumper, at the other end of the table. Whitney pulled up a chair and said, "Cable, I need some advice. Not exactly legal, but—"

"I'll be glad to help if I can," Jumper said.

"Well, I got a call from Regina's personal attorney this morning, asking me to come by his office. She'd left a letter with him a week or two before her death. Sealed. Addressed to me. It was—well, I can't think of another word for it— an accusation."

"Accusation?" Jumper repeated, looking alarmed.

"Yes. Very upsetting. She told me something about her life I hadn't known and expressed her concern that she might be in danger."

"From whom?"

"I'd rather not say right now. I don't know what to do. Regina might just have been imagining it all, and if I turn it over to the police—I don't know—they might jump to a conclusion that was only a suspicion on Regina's part."

"Whitney, you've *got* to give it to the police," Jumper said firmly. "They're not dummies. But if Regina really thought she was in danger from someone, she was probably right. If I were you, I'd call them immediately."

Whitney ran his hand through his tidy hair, an uncharacteristic movement. "Okay, okay. I guess I knew that's what you'd say. I know it's the right thing to do. It's just that—"

"It's the only thing you can do," Jumper said. "Do you want me to phone for you?"

"No. No, I'll call now."

"Use the phone in Regina's—I mean, Sharlene's—office. It's more private. I'll come with you if you want."

"No, thanks. I want to think about it a little more. I could be seriously harming someone. Thanks, Cable." With a weirdly formal handshake, he wandered off.

Jane assumed the pepper she was nibbling was probably good, but her mouth was so dry she could hardly swallow it. Shelley, sitting beside her, was nervously tapping her unused fork on the tablecloth. Time seemed to slow to a glacial pace as they sat there, unheard conversations washing over them.

"I can't stand this," Shelley whispered. "What if we're wrong?"

"We're not wrong," Jane said. "But if it doesn't work, we've just made fools of ourselves. It won't be the first time." Her voice shook with nerves.

They got up and took their plastic plates to the big wastebasket that had been set up by the front door, then moved slowly closer to the door to the staff area, where they stood silently for agonizing minutes.

Suddenly there were muffled sounds from behind the closed door. Shouts, scuffling, a door slamming. Jane clutched Shelley's hand and they stared at each other. There was a cry from behind the door, and it swung open.

Mel and a uniformed officer came through, each of them holding one of Lisa Quigley's arms. She was struggling weakly and sobbing incoherently. Mel looked at Jane and nodded.

As they threaded their way through the crowd, everyone fell deadly silent. Jane felt a hand on her arm and turned to see Babs, her face as white as the collar of her dress. "Where are they taking Lisa?" she asked.

"To jail," Jane answered sadly.

*   *   *

"... so **Whitney agreed** to stage that conversation with Jumper when he knew Lisa was listening?" Babs asked.

Babs, Sharlene, Shelley, and Jane were the only ones left at the museum. All the tables but one had been put away and they were sitting around it, finishing off the dregs of the coffee from the big urn.

"He and Jumper rehearsed it," Jane said.

"Then there really wasn't a letter from Regina?" Sharlene asked.

"Pure invention," Shelley replied. "But Lisa didn't know that. And she couldn't take the chance of Regina 'telling' the police who'd killed her. And Regina might have really written such a letter after Lisa wrote her that threatening note. The one you found in the dumpster, Sharlene."

"How did you ever figure this out?" Babs asked Jane.

"You and Shelley each figured half of it out," Jane said. "I just put the two halves together. You were talking to Jumper about passions and sex, and earlier, Shelley had suspected Whitney and said something about 'if I can't have her, nobody can.' She thought maybe Regina had finally decided not to marry him and he might have felt that way. In fact, it was the opposite. Regina had decided to commit herself to marriage, and it was Lisa who was the jealous lover. The Woman Scorned."

"Lover?" Sharlene said, a blush creeping up her throat. "Regina and Lisa were lesbians?"

Jane nodded. "But Regina must have been bisexual, forced to choose between two people she loved—one a man, one another woman. Once I thought of that, everything else fit and made sense in a horrible way. It was Lisa who set up the reenactment, you remember. We all saw it as a wonderful promotional gimmick, but Lisa meant it as a way to stage a murder in plain sight and cast suspicion on everyone else. Regina had waffled about marrying Whitney and if she'd decided to stay with Lisa, nothing would have happened at the reenactment. But when Regina said she and Whitney were going to announce their engagement at the groundbreaking, her fate was sealed."

"But what about Derek?" Sharlene asked. "What could he have possibly had to do with it?"

"Absolutely nothing," Jane said. "Poor jerk. He was mad at Jumper and made what he considered nasty remarks about a bunch of people. He said Jumper's friend the anchorwoman was frigid and that Regina was a lesbian. He was just throwing out excuses for why neither of them had fallen into his arms. But Lisa must have heard just the lesbian part and was afraid he knew something. What's more, even if he didn't, if he'd repeated it to enough people, eventually someone might take it seriously and realize the nature of their relationship and that there was a lot of about-to-be-thwarted passion to account for."

Babs stood up and took their empty coffee cups to the trash while Sharlene folded the tablecloth and Shelley and Jane folded up the table. "I still don't see what Heidi had to do with it, though," Sharlene said.

"Nothing," Jane said. "Remember that man who told you about the pea his family grew during the Depression? Caspar overheard the conversation and decided there might be seeds of it in the pea bin. That's why his fingerprints were all over it. But old Auguste had hidden the peas inside the cat. They might be valuable if they can be made to grow.

I had Mel take the stuffed cat and the ledger away just to keep them from Caspar."

"But why was Derek killed the way he was, then?"

"I'm not sure we'll ever know," Shelley said, looking daggers at the fingernail she'd just chipped on the folding table. "My guess is that Lisa lured him down to the basement somehow, smacked him in the head with something, then realized to her horror that he was merely unconscious, not dead. Maybe she couldn't bring herself to hit him again. Or maybe she was just plain crazy at that point. I imagine her eye fell on the pea bin and she figured if she stuffed his mouth and nose with peas, he'd suffocate. Maybe it even crossed her mind that doing that would confuse the time of death and allow her to establish an alibi. She hadn't taken time to carefully plan Derek's murder—well, who knows? She was desperate. She'd already killed her lover. She was terrified of getting caught, and terror can make anyone irrational."

"But there wasn't proof of anything," Jane said. "Which is why somebody had to try to lure Lisa into making another attempt to save herself."

"So Whitney and Jumper had that conversation at the table, where she could hear it," Babs mused. "To make her think the police were about to have reason to suspect her."

Jane nodded. "You have to admire Whitney for being willing to put himself at risk after learning something that must have been shocking to him."

"What happened in Ms. Palmer's office?" Sharlene asked.

"Your office, Sharlene," Babs corrected. "Didn't you get a call from your friend Detective VanDyne a few minutes ago, Jane?"

Jane nodded. "He said that Lisa grabbed the knife that had been used to slice that ham the volunteers bought for the dinner. She went into the office, sidled around behind Whitney, and tried to stab him. But there was one police officer in the closet, one crouched behind the file cabinet, and two more in the hall, so she never got close enough to nick Whitney. She went to pieces when the police grabbed her. She was at the breaking point and apparently confessed everything."

Sharlene picked up one end of the folded table and Jane the other. As they carried it over to where the other rented tables were stacked, Sharlene said, "I guess I must really be even more naive than I realized. It never crossed my mind that Ms. Palmer and Lisa were anything more than just good friends."

Babs was jingling the keys to the front door of the museum. "Are we done?" she asked. "Sharlene, don't feel bad for not realizing. In spite of today's openness, there are still many people who don't believe their sexual orientation is the business of the general public. Just like some people are secretive about their financial status, others feel that way about their sexual preferences. Still, I should have realized—"

"You?" Sharlene said with a smile. "Why should *you* of all people have realized?"

Babs shook her head and stared at Sharlene for a long moment. "My dear, you really are naive."

Sharlene stared back, her face a mask of perplexity; then her mouth dropped open in astonishment. "You mean—?"

"I do, indeed."

"You and Miss Daisy?"

Babs laughed. "My dear, why does the younger generation always think they invented sex? I remember feeling the same way at your age. I believe that's why Lisa locked me in the closet. She must have picked up on Daisy's and my 'special friendship'—that's what they called it when we were young women—and figured I was as well attuned as she was. She liked me too much to kill me on such a vague suspicion, but she was warning me to keep my opinions to myself. She might have even been telling me not to bring either of us 'out of the closet,' as they say."

Sharlene was still staring, openmouthed, and suddenly a giggle bubbled up. "For all the classes I've taken," she said, "I think I need to go back to kindergarten and start brushing up on the Facts of Life."

Babs grinned at her and headed for the door, opening it to usher the others out. As she locked up behind them, she said, "Can I give anyone a ride?"

"No, thanks," Sharlene said. "Jumper's waiting to take me home." She blushed only a little this time.

"And I'm taking Jane home," Shelley said.

Jane and Shelley walked slowly to Shelley's van while watching as Jumper leaped from a little, sporty car and chivalrously opened the door for Sharlene. Babs tooted her horn and waved as she passed. Shelley unlocked the van; after Jane got in and snapped her seat belt, she said, "Shelley, I'm disappointed."

"About what?" Shelley said, gunning the engine.

"Because I thought we *did* invent sex. In fact, I vividly remember inventing sex."

Shelley laughed and shot out into traffic like a rocket.